LAWLESS & TILLEY

Still Life

Kerry heard a car door opening behind her. The apparently empty vehicle that had been parked in the wood was not empty at all. A figure emerged and said, "Kerry, your dad sent me."

This person knew her name but Kerry did not recognize the mysterious driver. Confused, she asked hesitantly, "Who are you?"

"A friend of your dad." The stranger walked towards Kerry. "I've come to take you—"

Kerry did not wait for the end of the sentence. She was too suspicious. She turned her back and made for Copper. But she wasn't quick enough...

POINT CRIME

LAWLESS & TILLEY

Still Life

MALCOLM ROSE

SCHOLASTIC

Scholastic Children's Books
Commonwealth House, 1–19 New Oxford Street,
London WC1A 1NU, UK
a division of Scholastic Ltd
London ~ New York ~ Toronto ~ Sydney ~ Auckland

First published in the UK by Scholastic Ltd, 1998

Copyright © Malcolm Rose, 1998

ISBN 0 590 19858 0

Typeset by TW Typesetting, Midsomer Norton, Somerset
Printed by Cox & Wyman Ltd, Reading, Berks.

10 9 8 7 6 5 4 3 2 1

Kerry picked up a stick and pretended to throw it. Really, she didn't let go and instead hid it behind her back. Copper wasn't fooled. She always did that. He waited, gazing into her face, his tongue hanging out. "All right," Kerry said to him. "This time." She drew back her right arm and threw the stick as far as she could. Copper turned and bounded after it happily.

Copper was an eight-year-old Irish setter – a year older than Kerry. Kerry's dad would often joke, "We got a dog instead of you – because we couldn't afford a baby – but then you came along anyway!" Kerry had grown up with Copper. She loved him and thought of him as *her* dog. She always felt safe in the wood with him. Copper would never let her come to any harm. He was big and faithful and reddish-brown. "The colour of copper," her dad told her, explaining the dog's name. Her father was a chemist, so he should know. As she walked, Kerry twirled the dog's lead in her left hand.

Copper loped back to her with the trophy in his mouth. Dropping the slobbery stick at her feet was his way of dropping a hint. Eagerly, he gazed up into her face. Kerry picked it up by the dry end and threw it again, this time in the opposite direction. Copper galloped after it.

It was the early evening of a sizzling July day. The sun had lost none of its power, so it seemed much earlier than six o'clock. Kerry was feeling good because it was the first Monday of the summer break. No school for the next six weeks. She would be able to walk Copper through the wood at any time every day. Heaven. So much better than a stuffy classroom. She bent down and hugged Copper when he next delivered the stick, but Copper squirmed out of her arms. He was too keen on running and fetching to enjoy an embrace just now. Kerry laughed at him. "Oh, all right." She threw his beloved stick again.

This time, when Copper found it, he didn't grip it between his teeth and charge back to Kerry with it. He was taken with a nearby smell.

"Copper! Here, boy," Kerry called.

The dog didn't respond. He continued the investigation with his nose.

Kerry left the path and headed for Copper, muttering, "What have you found? Daft dog."

At school, Kerry was bright and popular. She was

good at games and was always willing to help anyone in her class with their work, so she had plenty of friends. Even when she wanted to get on with her own schoolwork, she'd stop to try and sort out someone else's problem if she was asked. And she never let on to the teacher if classmates claimed that they had done the work on their own. Kerry's best friend was Farida and their teacher would say, "You two make a good pair. You'll do really well – if you keep your minds on your work and off the nattering."

Kerry's hair was fair, almost blonde like her mother's – the exact opposite of Farida's flowing black hair. As Kerry walked towards Copper, her hair brushed against her shoulders. "Come on, Copper. Let's get going. Where's your stick?"

The stick had been forgotten. Copper was engrossed in something else. His nose seemed to be glued to it.

Kerry leaned on his back and looked down at his find. "What's –?" Then she cried, "Ugh!" and backed off, shouting, "Copper! That's disgusting! Come away."

The red setter was too intrigued with his discovery to obey her. He nudged it with his nose but the creature refused to react. Copper was surprised. Instead, he pushed it with his paw. It should have jumped up and run off or put up a fight. It did neither. It was dead. Reluctantly, perhaps disappointed, Copper abandoned his treasure and padded towards Kerry.

"How could you?" Kerry said to him. "I'm not going to let you lick me ever again – not after you've been round a dead rat."

Suddenly, two people jumped out from behind a couple of oaks. Scared and surprised, Kerry cried out. Copper started to bark ferociously.

With one hand over her heart and the other on her dog's back, Kerry murmured, "It's all right, Copper." To the two boys who had appeared and were giggling at the drastic effect that their prank had caused, she said, "Liam! Makbool! You're pests!" Makbool was Farida's older brother and Liam was his next-door neighbour. They were always messing around and getting into trouble at school.

Liam asked eagerly, "Did you say there's a dead rat? Where?"

Kerry made a tutting noise but waved her hand towards it anyway. "Over there."

"Great! Let's take a look," Liam said.

As they wandered towards it, Makbool said to his friend, "I bet it's all stiff."

"Perhaps it's got maggots," Liam put in enthusiastically.

Kerry left them to it, mumbling under her breath, "Boys!" When she started to walk again, she was tugged back. Her T-shirt had caught on a bramble. She released herself from its grip but only after pricking her finger and sacrificing a white thread of cotton to the barbed shrub. Once she had freed herself, she picked up another stick for Copper and resumed the game as she strolled through the wood.

At the edge of Hallam Golf Course, Copper dropped his stick. At the point where the dry-stone wall was low enough for him to see over, his keen eyes picked out something much tastier. He jumped over the stones and made for the small white ball that rolled towards one of the greens. Simultaneously, two people shouted. Kerry's familiar voice ordered, "No, Copper! Leave it. Come here." A man in outlandish checked trousers yelled threateningly and, angrily brandishing a club, hurtled towards the dog. Faced with such fierce opposition, Copper gave up chasing the ball, jumped back over the wall and returned to Kerry.

The path at the perimeter of the golf course held a hundred fascinating smells. Kerry did not notice but Copper's sensitive nose caught them all and his unending curiosity compelled him to investigate each one. Frequently, Kerry called, "Oh, come on, Copper." She made her way cautiously down the steep path on to the rough track that would take her to the road. Approaching the end of the track, Kerry put Copper back on his lead.

On the pavement beside the quiet road, she saw an old man stumble over a crooked slab and fall to the ground, the shopping in his bag scattering all over the place.

Kerry had been taught to be wary of strangers, but she had also been encouraged to be kind and use her head. The majority of people were harmless, ordinary and trustworthy. Kerry could not imagine that this old man, sitting on the pavement and rubbing his elbows, could pose any sort of threat to her. Besides, there was no one else about to help him. There was a car, parked on the dirt track in the wood, but the driver was nowhere to be seen. Strangely, though, the boot lid seemed to be raised slightly as if it was not properly shut. Kerry looped Copper's lead over a fence post and said, "Stay there a minute. Wait, there's a good boy." She squatted by the old man and asked, "Are you all right?"

The old man groaned, "I'm getting too old for this. But if you'll help me up, my dear, I'll be fine."

Kerry took one of his arms and pulled as he clambered to his feet.

Once upright, he groaned again and glanced back accusingly at the paving stone. "It's a disgrace! I'd write to the council and complain but with my hands…" In explanation, he held out a bony, shaky hand, probably incapable of writing legibly. "Oh well, that's life, I suppose."

Kerry was not sure how to offer sympathy, so instead, she picked up his bag and began to collect his goods, which were littering the pavement. Concerned about her absence, Copper barked. Kerry called in return, "Won't be long."

Peering into the wood, the man said, "Your dog? You won't let him off, will you? He sounds ferocious."

Kerry stood up with a packet of biscuits, almost

certainly reduced to crumbs, and replied, "Oh, he's not. He protects me but he's not nasty." She placed the packet in the bag and looked around for any more spilled items. The old man had lost interest. He let Kerry get on with the job of gathering together his shopping. At the kerb, a big black beetle was investigating his tube of toothpaste. Kerry didn't like creepy-crawlies. She shivered, hesitated and then quickly snatched the toothpaste away from the bug. When she couldn't see any more scattered purchases, she went up to the pensioner and held out his bag.

Still feeling sore, the old man took it from her and said, "Thank you, my dear. That's your good deed for the day done. I wish there were more like you."

Kerry smiled and asked, "Will you be OK now?"

He nodded, with a pained expression on his face. Perhaps he was hinting that Kerry should carry his shopping home for him, but he said, "I think so. I'll be getting on. You'd better get back to that dog of yours."

"All right," Kerry replied, and headed for the track where Copper was waiting anxiously.

The dog's eyes brightened and he wagged his tail enthusiastically when Kerry returned. As she got within a few metres of Copper, Kerry halted. She heard a car door opening behind her. The apparently empty vehicle that had been parked in the wood was not empty at all. A figure emerged and said, "Kerry, your dad sent me."

This person knew her name but Kerry did not

recognize the mysterious driver. Confused, she asked hesitantly, "Who are you?"

"A friend of your dad." The stranger walked towards Kerry. "I've come to take you—"

Kerry did not wait for the end of the sentence. She was too suspicious. She turned her back and made for Copper. But she wasn't quick enough. She felt a strong arm around her body and a hand clamped over her mouth. Her cry was stifled and she was bundled towards the boot.

Aware that all was not well with Kerry, Copper snarled and lunged at her captor. Still attached to the fence post, however, Copper was stopped by his lead. He let out a bark.

Too shocked at first to put up much of a fight, Kerry was dumped into the boot. When she started to thrash about with her hands, they were gripped tightly and bound with cord. Her legs were too confined in the cramped space to kick out. She cried, "No! Help!" Almost immediately, foul tape was slapped across her mouth and any further yells were reduced to useless grunts.

Copper grew frantic. With all his strength, he yanked against the post that restrained him while the driver slammed down the lid of the boot and moved towards the car door. Copper tugged and the post began to give way, churning up the ground at its base. Under pressure, it leaned more and more. After one final, desperate lunge, Copper's lead slipped off the post and the furious dog dashed round the car towards the stranger who had taken Kerry. Before the door closed, Copper's jaws clamped tightly round the bottom of the driver's lightweight jacket. His back legs locked and he pulled tenaciously, as if he were playing tug-of-war with Kerry's father and a rubber ring. He never lost that game. He pulled with a determined growl in his throat. The person in the car grabbed the jacket and tried to jerk it away from the red setter. Copper resisted. The driver decided to slam the door shut anyway, knowing it would bang the dog's head.

As the door flew at him, Copper ducked but bravely kept a grip on the coat. There was a ripping noise, the material tore and the door crashed shut. The car snarled into life. As it accelerated on to the road, turned right and sped away, Copper was left with a mouthful of polyester. With a pitiful whine, he watched the car containing Kerry speeding down the road. He disentangled the sizeable piece of grey material from his teeth, dropped it and sniffed around, trying to decide what to do. After a few minutes of exploring Kerry's lingering smell where the car had been parked, he made for home.

Brett Lawless, whose rank of Detective Inspector had been confirmed after his arrest of the serial killer dubbed the Messenger, took a drink from the ice-cold can and sighed. He wasn't weary after trouncing his old university friend at squash but, in deference to Phil, who was still sweating, he pretended to be more tired than he actually was. "Good game," he said.

"Mmm." His opponent nodded. "I suppose it's all that chasing after crooks that keeps you so fit. If you'd continued with chemistry like me, you'd have been stuck behind benches and desks for so long, you wouldn't be so quick on your feet."

Brett laughed. "You've been watching too much telly. Policing is mainly mind-numbing paperwork, you know. Computers and reports. I'll tell you one thing, though. If I'd carried on with chemistry I'd be earning a lot more, that's for sure."

Phil took a gulp from his own can. "Yeah, but you wouldn't have it any other way. You look every inch the cop now. You've found your niche. Not exactly rolling in money, but almost saintly. Out of your probationary period and one of the stars of that serial-killer case."

For an instant, Brett frowned. He was thinking of another star of that case – his partner, Clare Tilley – and her treatment by the selection board. To change the subject, he asked, "How's the hydrogen car going? *Is* it still going?"

Phil put down his drink on the table as if he were about to deliver a serious lecture. "It certainly is. *Very* well – just like I said it would. I'm about to join the ranks of you media stars. I'm going to change the image of the car from major environmental hazard to friendly cuddly creature that everyone loves. All cars are going to be green! Lorries and planes as well, I think."

Phil Chapman was just as competitive in his profession as he was on the squash court. He worked for the company H-Cars, and he was responsible for the breakthrough that would allow hydrogen to be stored and used as a clean fuel in cars. In a world that many believed was being warmed alarmingly by the burning of petrol or diesel in vehicles, the pollution-free hydrogen car offered a solution and a reprieve for the Earth. Of course, it also offered astronomical profits for the manufacturer. Along with the world, wealth was at stake. Phil was torn between his natural inclination to celebrate his sensational research and H-Cars' requirement for secrecy to protect the invention. Never one to keep quiet about his achievements, Phil itched to share his success. He had already boasted about it to Brett, knowing that his friend would be interested yet discreet with the information. Unwisely, though, he had also bragged about his environment-saving research when other people might have been listening.

Phil's mobile phone chirped like a hungry young bird demanding to be fed. He reached into his sports bag and took it out. "Yes?" he said with a degree of impatience, because he assumed that someone at work was intruding on his precious free time. Immediately, his face creased and he listened more carefully. After a minute, he said, "OK. Just try and stay cool. Calm down. I'm on my way. Yes."

Brett put down his drink. "What is it? Trouble?"

Phil shrugged as he gathered his things together. "Some panic at home. Something about Kerry taking the dog out for a walk and the dog arriving back without her. I'd better go and sort it out."

"Sure," Brett said, concerned. "Want me to come?"

"No, it's OK. Probably nothing. I bet Kerry's back before I get there. Besides, I'm sure you've got other things to do. Baddies to hunt." Phil slung his bag over his shoulder and said, with a feigned threat, "Next time, I'll beat you."

Brett smiled. "Maybe," he said. He called after his retreating friend, "Hope it's all right at home. I'll call."

An hour later, Brett phoned Phil from home. "Is everything all right? Is Kerry OK?"

Hesitantly, Phil replied, "Er, yeah. It was nothing."

Immediately, Brett realized that his friend was holding back. "Sure? What happened?" he prompted.

"Oh, Kerry and Copper got separated," Phil said evasively. "That's all."

Brett could not imagine Copper deserting Kerry. Changing tack to get at the truth and imagining that Phil's wife might have panicked, Brett asked, "Is Chloe OK?"

"She's fine," Phil answered.

"And Kerry's back now, is she?"

For a moment, there was an ominous silence. It was as though emotion was being controlled. Then Phil muttered, "Yes." His tone was broken.

"Come clean, Phil. What's the problem?"

"Nothing. It's OK."

"Doesn't sound like nothing. I'd better come round."

"No," Phil snapped, as if a life depended on it. "No need. Anyway, I've got to go now."

Brett was left with a hum in his ear and a worried frown on his face. He was sure that his friend was lying to him. Suddenly restless, Brett strolled across his living room and stood by the window, but he noticed little outside. He didn't see the boys playing football in the quiet street, his neighbour's new car, a black cat strolling across his lawn as if it owned the place. Instead, Brett turned to his aquarium and leaned on its edge. The sleek tropical fish rose excitedly, anticipating food. Brett gazed into the water distractedly. He was thinking about Kerry rather than feeding the fish. He was wondering what had gone wrong.

Unable to settle, Brett went to his fridge and took out a cold beer. By the time that he'd gulped it down, the phone rang again. It was Phil, and he was speaking in an unfamiliar whisper. "Brett, I just... You're a cop. I need some advice. Nothing else, just advice. All right?"

Brett sighed. "Look, Phil, you've got me worried. If anything's happened to Kerry—"

Phil interrupted, "It's not a good idea for you to get involved."

"I *am* involved. You know that. Sounds like you need a friend."

At first, there was no response. Then Phil mumbled, "I appreciate your... But I just need—"

There was a scream in the background. "Phil! Don't you dare!" It must have been loud because Brett heard it clearly and recognized Chloe's voice.

"Phil, what *is* going on? Tell me or I'm on my way, right now."

But at the other end of the line Phil was talking to Chloe. "I'm just asking Brett for advice."

"No!" Chloe snapped. "Keep him out of it."

Brett kept his ear to the receiver. He had never heard Chloe so agitated before, even hysterical. Then he caught Phil's anguished response. "We've got a problem, Chloe. I don't know what else to do. I'm desperate. We haven't got much choice. Brett might be able to help. He's a good mate and he loves Kerry."

Chloe said, "I know. But remember what it said. You can't bring him into this."

Brett frowned because he didn't understand.

"I can't just sit here," Phil cried. "I've got to do *something*. She's my daughter too, and I need to talk to Brett about it."

There was some sobbing, a long pause and a stifled exchange before Chloe said more softly, "All right, then. But if you risk Kerry..." Either she did not finish her threat or Brett did not detect it.

"Brett?" It was Phil's voice again.

"Yes," he replied. "I'm still here."

"Look, I can't break this gently. It *is* Kerry. She's been kidnapped."

Brett was stunned. "Kidnapped?" He struggled to act like a police officer trained to deal dispassionately with crime when he felt sickened. "Are you sure, Phil? She's not just lost? How do you know?" Kerry was such a warm girl. Wouldn't hurt a fly. Brett could not believe that someone might want to make her suffer.

Phil stammered, "She disappeared while she was walking Copper in the wood. Now we've had a note pushed through the door. It says we mustn't contact the police. That's why we … you know."

Brett was horrified. "I'm coming over," he announced.

"No!" Phil cried. "They might be watching. If you come, they'll know."

"Not every caller has to be from the police, Phil. I'll come as a friend, not a police officer. Surely, you want me to lend a hand."

"Yes, but Chloe won't have it. And remember you look every inch a policeman. Even when you're not on duty."

Brett knew what he meant. Certain groups of people, like police officers and university students, were as easy to spot as fish. No matter what its shape, size, colour and age, a fish always looked like a fish – from the dwarf pygmy goby to the whale shark. Police officers were just as easy to recognize – any time, any place. "All right," Brett said into the phone. Still determined to help, he added, "But you know how I feel about Kerry. There's a way round this. I'll bring someone with me. A woman. We'll make it look like a couple visiting. Then I won't look like a cop."

Phil paused. He seemed to be on the point of relenting. "Who is she? Another detective?"

"Yes. Clare Tilley. But we can put on a pretty good show of being a couple when we want to," Brett promised, anticipating that Clare would agree to his scheme. "Just friends visiting. That's what it'll look like. Perfectly natural."

16

"Well, we could do with someone to talk it through with." Phil hesitated and then continued, "All right. Make it convincing, though, won't you? I can't let anything happen to Kerry."

"Neither can I," Brett put in firmly. "I'll be careful."

"I'll talk to Chloe, try and calm her down, while you get over here."

Brett rang Clare's home number immediately but only got her answering machine. He tried her mobile phone instead. When she answered, he said, "It's me. Emergency. Where are you?"

"I'm off duty," she replied. "Ever heard of it?"

"If only. But this is different. Remember my mate, Phil Chapman?"

Clare had a phenomenal memory. "Your university friend. Chemist. Good squash player, but not quite good enough."

"That's him. This is about his daughter." He told Clare everything he knew about Kerry's disappearance.

"OK," Clare said, without further objection or delay. "I'm on my way."

"So, where are you?"

"Promise you won't laugh?"

"I'm not in the mood," Brett retorted.

"I'm getting away from it all." Her tone hovered between scorn and good humour. "A bit of peace and quiet in the art gallery. Right now, three people are scowling at me for disturbing them."

"Up by the university?"

"Yeah. I can be at your place in ten minutes."

"It's a deal," Brett said. "Thanks, Clare. Sorry to drag—"

Clare interrupted him wryly. "I don't expect anything else. I'm a police officer. Even if only a lowly sergeant."

"And, through me, a friend to the Chapmans. That's what you are tonight. A friend, not a detective."

"You got it."

It was an unsettling experience. Clare's left arm stretched behind his back and her hand gripped his waist. Brett's right arm was draped round her shoulders. He had not held a woman like that for a year – since his girlfriend had died. It was a sham to be strolling to Phil's house arm in arm with his partner, yet, because he and Clare enjoyed each other's company, it did not seem like make-believe. Acting was difficult but this seemed easy. Brett experienced a curious mixture of pleasure and embarrassment while he held her.

Sensing his dilemma, Clare taunted him as they walked up Phil's drive. "Mmm. I could get used to this." Then she smiled wickedly.

They arrived at the door before Brett could respond.

Almost as soon as Brett rang the bell, Phil appeared and dragged them off the doorstep.

Immediately, Brett and Clare parted, like illicit lovers caught redhanded. They were police officers again.

In the living room, Chloe was utterly distraught. Her eyes were red from crying. Clare went to her straightaway and introduced herself. "We've come to help," she said. "To do whatever we can."

"Did anyone see you?" she asked.

"Even if they did, we just looked like casual visitors. We couldn't have looked less like police officers," Clare answered. "No damage done."

The red setter was lying at Chloe's feet. He was resting his head miserably on his paws and occasionally he issued a whimper. He kept on looking up at Chloe and Phil, moving his eyes and not his head. The expression was particularly doleful – as if he'd just been punished for wolfing the family's evening meal while no one was looking. He certainly had the air of a dog who had done something seriously wrong. But the blame was self-imposed. Phil and Chloe were sure that Copper would have tried his best to save Kerry. They were only disappointed that he couldn't talk about the awful event in the wood.

Brett looked at Phil and then at Chloe. "You'd better tell us all about it."

"We always thought Kerry was safe when she went out with Copper," Chloe blurted.

"We didn't think anyone would try anything with a big dog around," Phil added.

"You almost sound as if you expected someone to try something," Brett said. "Is that right?"

Phil answered, "No, not really. Just that, these days, you hear such a lot about violent crime."

"I imagine Copper would have had a go at anyone trying to take Kerry away. Agreed?" asked Brett.

"Almost certainly."

"And did she take him on the same route every time she walked him?"

"More or less."

Brett nodded. "What was she wearing?" he enquired, looking at Chloe.

"Just a plain white T-shirt and black trousers." Chloe wept – it was the sort of question that police officers, not friends, asked.

Clare was still thinking about the Chapmans' surprise that their daughter might be targeted. She probed gently. "Do you know anyone who *might* have a reason for taking Kerry? In most of these cases, the family knows the culprit."

The Chapmans glanced at each other before Phil answered, "Well, I suppose we've had our worries. Nothing definite, you understand."

"What?" Clare queried.

"It's this job of mine," Phil replied. "I think word's out that I've cracked the problem of safely storing hydrogen in cars. It's hard to overestimate its importance. Lots of manufacturers would like to get in on the act. I've been approached by three different companies: one wanting to lure me away from H-Cars, another offering sackfuls of money for my method, and another virtually threatening me."

"Threatening?"

Phil shrugged. "I didn't take it seriously. They just said I should come over to their side or I'd regret it."

"Who was it?" asked Clare.

"Ross Mundee of Sabre."

"And who were the other two?" Brett enquired.

"A vehicle engineer called Alan Fox from Morlands in Barnsley, and Hilary Garner, boss of Ventura. That's in Coventry."

Brett said, "I'm sorry, Phil, but I have to ask. Did you encourage these people in any way? Did you go for these bribes, or promise anything to stop the intimidation?"

"I'm perfectly happy at H-Cars," Phil replied. "They're paying me well enough. I don't need extra cash incentives. I'm into saving the world, Brett, not making a fortune. And a bit of intimidation won't stop me."

Chloe flashed a reproachful look at her husband from behind the handkerchief that she was holding to her face and chewing nervously. "You've got more than a *bit* of intimidation now."

Clare put in, "Brett said you'd got a note."

Chloe forced herself up to go and fetch it from the table. Copper slunk out of her way. Brett called after her, "We'll come and look. Don't touch it more than you have already. I want to take it away for tests."

Together, Clare and Brett huddled over the folded piece of paper. It was a brief note, written neatly in blue ink.

*I have Kerry. You will recieve instructions later —
after you have felt what it's like to be incomplete. Do not
involve the police.*

"Not a great speller," Brett observed, pointing at
"recieve". "And no direct threat about the police, just
an order. When did you get it?"

"Not sure," Chloe replied. "I saw it after Copper
came back – and after I called you, Phil."

"Quarter to seven," Brett muttered.

"So you didn't see who delivered it?" Clare asked.

Chloe shook her head and started to sob.

Clare touched her arm and decided to give her
something to do. She guessed that Kerry's mother
might feel better if she was being useful. "Find a
clean plastic bag, Chloe. Slip the paper into the bag
but handle it just by the edges, OK? Then stay here,
in case you get another message."

Brett nodded in agreement. "I'll arrange for your
phone calls to be traced and recorded. I want to know
who phones you and from where."

"Where are you going?" Chloe asked frantically.

"Into the wood," Brett replied. "We need to retrace
Kerry's steps. There could be all sorts of evidence in
the place where she was taken."

"But—" Chloe began to protest.

"If we're going to get to the bottom of this, we've
got to poke around, Chloe," Brett put in quickly.
"No one'll see us in the wood anyway," he added
reassuringly. "But taking a look there is the natural
thing to do. You've invited round a couple of mates

to scour the wood for Kerry. Nothing to do with the police."

"All right," Chloe agreed. "Just don't go out looking like police."

"We won't," Brett promised.

"You look so calm about all this." In her distressed state, Chloe's comment to Brett sounded like an accusation of not caring.

"Only on the outside, Chloe," Brett muttered, hiding his pain.

"I suppose you want me to come," Phil said. "Show you where she usually goes."

"That's right," Brett confirmed. "And would Copper be able to lead us, do you think?"

"Probably," Phil replied. "But why?"

"Perhaps he'll react in some way when he gets to the spot where Kerry was kidnapped. We need him to identify it for us."

"All right. Worth a try, I suppose."

Then Chloe said to her husband, "While you're out, Phil, you'd better tell them about that weird woman as well. You never know."

Puzzled, both Brett and Clare looked at Phil.

Phil's head drooped, but he consented, with a groan. Then he went to fetch Copper's leash.

Sunset was three-quarters of an hour away. It was no longer hot in the Sheffield wood but the light was still good. This time, Copper did not prance joyfully from tree to tree. He seemed to realize that he had a job to do. He kept to the usual path, guiding them faithfully along the route that he had taken earlier with Kerry.

While they walked, Phil asked, "Well? What can you do to help?"

Brett considered his reply for a moment and then said, "For one thing, we can examine that note."

Interrupting, Phil said, "Does handwriting analysis work?"

Brett shrugged. "Sometimes. But it's not good enough to rely on. No, I meant ESDA. Electrostatic detection apparatus. It'll show up any impressions left from writing on the previous page. That might give us something. And we'll check with all the local doctors and hospitals for anyone treated for a dog bite this evening."

"We should ask around your neighbourhood in case anyone saw who delivered that note," Clare interjected, even though she knew that Phil would object.

"But that'll make it obvious we've been in touch with the police! It could risk Kerry's life. Chloe would go crazy."

"We know. First, we'll sneak someone from surveillance into your house," Brett said. "That'll soon tell us if you're being watched. If not, we can move a bit more freely. But we'll need some forensic back-up straightaway if we find the place where Kerry was abducted."

Phil sighed. He wanted progress, he wanted action, but he didn't want to jeopardize his daughter. He didn't want to provoke the writer of the note. He was frustrated and scared.

"You'd better tell us about this mystery woman, Phil," Brett said as they paused while Copper smelled the remains of a dead rat.

"I suppose so." He swallowed and said, "It started about nine months ago."

"Just a second," Brett interrupted. He was watching Copper, who had begun to sniff at a bush, then cast his sad eyes significantly towards Phil. Brett peered at the bramble and said, "Here's something! A thread – with a red stain." Glancing at Phil, he continued, "Could be blood, I'm afraid. I daren't leave it till we get a scene-of-the-crime team. It might blow away. Has either of you got a clean hankie?"

"A tissue," Clare replied, handing it to her partner.

Brett laid the strand on the tissue, wrapped it up and then pulled it off the bush. He put the evidence carefully in his pocket, then took a stick and shoved it in the ground to mark the spot.

Phil watched him with a dismal expression, as if his friend were marking a grave with a makeshift cross. "So, this is what police work's like. Just another case to you."

Brett grimaced. "It's more than that to me, Phil. You know it is. But I won't help you – or Kerry – by showing how angry I am. I'm trying to keep my head."

"Do you think this was where she was kidnapped?" Phil muttered.

"No," Brett answered. "It's too far from the road to make a quick getaway. I can't imagine anyone dragging a girl kicking and screaming, with a dog barking and snapping, through the rest of the wood. Let's crack on before the light begins to fade. And you were telling us about the woman Chloe mentioned."

"That's right," Phil began again. "I went on local TV and contributed to a debate on pollution. Chloe says it all started after that. She thinks this woman –

about thirty, quite good-looking – must have seen me on the programme and got interested in me. She started to follow me to work and back. Embarrassing really, and annoying. Sometimes she'd wait outside work or home, just staring through the windows. I'm convinced she stayed outside our house all night on more than one occasion. And I've seen her with a camera, so I think she's taken photos of me for some reason. I got stupid gifts delivered as well. Things I hadn't ordered, nor had Chloe. You know: ties, flowers, shirts, meals. Even the odd lock of hair. And we got phone calls at home. No one would speak but I could tell there was someone on the line, listening. I could just hear the breathing. Definitely female. I think it was the same woman."

"Seems that you've got yourself a stalker, Phil," Clare said. "Just to add to your problems. But you make it sound as if it's in the past."

"I haven't seen her hanging around for a good few days."

"You never mentioned this to me before." Brett believed that his friend should have confided in him earlier.

Phil shrugged. "I didn't want to make a big deal of it. I blotted her out, hoping she'd go away. Perhaps now it's worked. Besides, I had more important things on my mind, more interesting things to talk about."

"I think you're right, Phil," Clare said in his defence. "Any response from you – even confronting her and telling her to get lost – would've fed her obsession with you."

"We'll need her description," Brett told him. "Tomorrow, I'll send an artist to work with you to get a likeness of her."

Phil nodded desolately.

"Do you know her name or where she comes from?"

"Sorry. No idea."

They'd reached the edge of the golf course and Copper began to pull on the lead impatiently. Phil frowned and then glanced at Brett. "Copper's trying to tell us something. It's along this path, I bet."

They dropped down on to the track. Near the road, Copper suddenly stopped and sat down. He looked up at his master and whined. Brett and Clare did not need a translator. The dog's expression was perfectly eloquent.

Brett looked at his jaded friend and said, "Decision time, Phil. One phone call and I can have this place secured. Stop any evidence from being taken, obliterated or contaminated, or washed away if it rains. I can have lights and a team here in a few minutes. I recommend it. As a friend as well as a police officer. The clues that lead us to Kerry might be here right now."

"So might the person who wrote the note."

"I doubt it," Clare ventured. "They'll be with Kerry, or watching somewhere near the house. They wouldn't see a few forensic scientists scrabbling around here."

Phil shook his head. "I can't risk it. You'd know if it was your daughter."

"OK," Brett said. "But let's not trample all over the place anyway. You see, Phil, if a car pulled in here, there could be tracks. If they're clear, a forensic team might be able to narrow it down to a particular make of car by the wheel–to–wheel distance. And if a car's got four identical tyres, it usually means they're the originals supplied by the makers. In other words, the car's fairly new. Useful information."

Clare chipped in, "Look. We've got a leaning fence post here. It's been yanked recently because it's pulled up fresh earth. Knocked in a struggle, perhaps."

Brett squatted down and murmured, "That's not all." He pointed a few metres ahead and said, "There's some torn cloth there. Grey. I'm going to have to take a look now, in case it blows away. Have you got any more tissues, Clare?"

Kneeling down gingerly by the find, Brett added, "If I'm any judge, I'd say it's got teeth marks on it. With a bit of luck, it was Copper and he's salvaged us a good clue."

"Any tyre impressions?" Clare enquired from a distance.

"Several, unfortunately. Quite a few cars have pulled on to this track. I can't tell if any are fresh." Brett stood up and gazed at his friend through the gloom of twilight. "Phil, we're hardly scratching the surface here. I don't need to tell you, a scientist, the difference between a quick look-see and a proper investigation. We need a photographer and the rest of the forensic crew. Think about it, for Kerry's sake."

Phil was torn between his daughter's welfare, his wife's frenzy and the needs of a thorough inquiry. Miserably, he said, "Chloe blames me for all this, you know. Me and my work. If you're not careful, she'll blame you for being a cop."

"If we're going to get through this, Phil, we're going to have to pull together, not blame each other." In an attempt to persuade his friend, Brett proposed, "I can camouflage the examination. No police vehicles, uniforms or ribbon. It'll look like they're surveying the place."

"At this time of night?"

Brett shrugged. "I'm not sure I can offer anything else. We're well away from the house, though," he pointed out. "Well away from prying eyes."

"I still don't think Chloe would stand for it."

Brett spread his arms. "All I know is, a good forensic examination might tell us who's got Kelly. Would you or Chloe want to miss out on that?"

Phil let out a long breath while he scanned the deserted site. Then he made up his mind. "OK, Brett. But be careful. Very careful."

Brett nodded. "I think it's the right decision, Phil."

* * *

Keith Johnstone had secured the post of Chief Constable in another force. He'd been replaced in the South Yorkshire Police force by Detective Chief Superintendent John Macfarlane. A year ago, after supervising Brett's first major case, Big John had moved to North Wales Police and been promoted. He did not mix well with Wales and he ached to return to Sheffield, where he had a reputation as formidable as his sizeable figure. Keith Johnstone's departure gave him that opportunity and he was welcomed back with open arms.

Brett could not recall seeing his bulky superior sitting behind a desk before. But he remembered his temper when people or events conspired against him. "So," John was saying in a cynical tone, "you just cracked on with it – this missing girl – before a case was even established. You know I like initiative, Brett, but not unofficial investigations. What happened to normal procedure, case management and conventional allocation of investigating officers?"

"Phil Chapman's a friend. His daughter's—"

"I appreciate you have personal involvement. But you presumed I'd put you in charge. Why should I? You're not exactly detached from this case, are you?"

Brett shook his head. "No, sir. Not at all."

"It's a very serious crime. You realize that any abduction of a girl under sixteen contravenes the Sexual Offences Act, don't you?" His eyebrows rose.

"Yes, but I didn't think it necessary to tell her

parents that. It could've raised even more ugly possibilities in their minds. Unnecessary at this stage."

"Well, I suppose that suggests you might have the sensitivity to take this case on," Big John admitted.

"I think so," Brett ventured.

"I'm more persuaded by the fact that Clare'll hold your hand, and keep you in check."

"Are you saying we can crack on, sir?"

John sat back and exhaled loudly, like a balloon leaking air. "It *does* feel like a case for you. Scientists at each other's throats. It suits your strengths so, against my better judgment, I'm giving it to you, yes. But watch your step, both of you. I'm uneasy with this one. I always get a bad feeling when young girls disappear. Such cases often develop into seriously messy business. Emotionally charged, sad, despicable. You'll have your hands full dealing with the parents, and the press if they get hold of it, as well as finding the culprit. I'm giving it to you because, one, there's the science connection and, two, you're well placed to handle the parents." He paused before adding, "You can have the resources you need tonight. I'll assign the rest of your back-up tomorrow, when you've got more of an idea what's needed. Now, go and sort it out before it gets messier than it is already."

In the corridor, Clare slapped her partner on the back. "My calming influence, eh? Where would you be without it?" When Brett opened his mouth to reply, Clare said quickly, "Don't answer that!"

As she drove back to the wood where Brett had

installed the disguised scene-of-the-crime team, Clare said, "Phil and Chloe must have had Kerry quite young – while Phil was still at university."

"Yeah," Brett replied. "Phil met Chloe while he was still in the first year. In fact, I was there. We went to a gig at the Leadmill. It sounds cringy but I think it was a case of love at first sight. Phil left student accommodation pretty quickly as I recall. Went to live with Chloe. He carried on with his course and she provided the money, working at a vet's. She loved animals. Still does. It was Chloe who got Copper. He was someone's unwanted Christmas present, a puppy abandoned outside the vet's. Chloe persuaded Phil to give him a home. Then Kerry came along – unplanned. She was the catalyst. Phil and Chloe decided to tie the knot. And they've been happily married ever since, as far as I know."

It was ten-fifteen when Clare pulled up by the side of the road. With Brett she got out of the car and peered up and down the street. The remnants of twilight were giving way to nightfall. There were no signs of onlookers taking an unhealthy interest in the unusual activities in the locality of the kidnap. The rest of the road was eerily quiet.

The scene itself looked like something out of a science-fiction film. Sinister government agents could have been studying an alien landing site at the edge of the wooded parkland. Behind orange tape, unidentified workers scavenged under glaring spotlights for anything out of the ordinary. To the outsider, their painstaking examinations might look like mystic rituals.

At the anonymous ribbon, Brett was pleased to see Greta, the senior forensic scientist. He greeted her quietly and queried her progress.

Neither optimistic nor pessimistic, Greta said, "A lot of work here. Ninety per cent is probably irrelevant, of course. We've got a leaning post, four soft-drink cans, a couple of plastic bottles, that piece of cloth you mentioned, a syringe, a chewed stick, tyre impressions of several cars, and dozens of other items. It's going to be a long job, through the night here and a lot of time in the lab. But I'll make sure it's a good job."

"I know you will," Brett replied, smiling at her.

Greta chose not to divulge the fact that she loathed crimes against children so much that she had put herself in charge. "You know the kid?" she asked.

Brett nodded bitterly. "Yeah. She's seven years old, Greta. She should be back with her folks. That's where she belongs."

"I'll put all this stuff at the top of the pile."

"Thanks," Brett said. "You'll have to prioritize. The cloth, definitely. And that syringe. Sounds worrying. Anything left in it to identify?"

"Not a lot. Slight residue, though, so it shouldn't be a big problem."

"I really need to track down any cars in the vicinity, so you could put those tyre treads near the top of the list as well."

"Sure," Greta agreed. "That piece of material, by the way, is probably polyester, and I think you're right about the canine tooth marks. I'll need to get a dental specialist into the Chapmans' to get an impression of their dog's teeth, OK? Can you tell them and get it organized? I understand we've got to tread softly near the house."

Brett nodded. "Your specialist may have to look like a casual caller."

"Fair enough. If the marks match their dog's, it's your best piece of evidence, once I get the traces done in the lab. And there might be another good find." Greta produced a small plastic bag containing an unopened packet of pills. "Lurking under the hedge by the pavement, over there. Out of view."

Brett took the evidence bag and muttered, "Zantac tablets." He looked at Greta and said, "OK, we've got a potential suspect or witness with ulcers."

"That's right. Unfortunately, it's an over-the-counter product now. If it was still a prescription drug, you'd have the owner's name and address on the packet."

Clare said, "There's an all-night chemist's shop down the road, just round the corner. Perhaps that's where it came from."

Brett glanced at Clare and then back to Greta. "Can I take them for the moment?" Seeing her nod, he said to Clare, "Come on, then. Let's go to the shop and find out. Straightaway. Ask if they remember anyone buying Zantac earlier, before they forget today's clients."

*   *   *

The man serving in Waters Pharmacy frowned as he squinted at Brett's ID. "Zantac, you say?"

Brett produced the packet, sealed in its evidence bag, and dangled it in front of the pharmacist.

"It's a best-seller in the pharmaceutical hit parade," he declared. "I dare say we sold a few today."

"Can you check?"

"Personally, no. The supervisor knows how to do these things electronically. She's in first thing in the morning."

Clare asked, "Have you been on duty during normal hours today?"

"No. I'm the night shift. Lucky me."

"Can you call one of your colleagues, the supervisor perhaps, and check what they remember about Zantac sales today?"

The pharmacist looked at his watch pointedly.

"A little girl has been abducted and whoever bought this packet," Brett said authoritatively, "might be able to help our inquiries. I think that takes precedence over a good night's sleep."

Intimidated by Brett's vehemence, the man relented and went to a back room to make the call. From the shop, Brett and Clare could only make out snatches of the pharmacist's conversation. When he returned, he was smiling. "Good news. It was almost certainly bought by a Mr Hobson. A regular client. Somewhat doddery. We're well used to him. How can I put it? It's no great surprise when he misplaces things."

"Why are you so sure it's him? Just because he loses things?"

"No. Apparently, he came in twice today. He bought the Zantac on the first visit. On the second, late in the evening, he bought some more to replace the ones he'd lost."

Brett and Clare glanced at each other. Their luck was holding, so far. "Hobson," Brett repeated. "Do you know where he lives?"

"If he got them on prescription, we'd have his address, but he didn't, so we don't. But he's local. First name of Harry."

"Thanks very much," Brett replied. "That's helpful. Can I borrow your telephone directory before we leave you in peace?"

Fortunately, there was an entry for a H M Hobson in Bayheath Road, so Brett and Clare set out immediately. It was less than a couple of minutes away by car.

Harry Hobson's bungalow was in darkness. Perhaps, like most of the people in the road, he had retired to bed. Even so, Brett pressed the doorbell insistently. He could not rest until he had found his friend's daughter.

Eventually the hall light came on and the front door opened just a crack. The old man's voice filtered out, "What's going on? Do you know what time it is? Who is it?"

Brett could hardly see anything through the small gap, only a door chain and a sliver of Mr Hobson in his dressing gown. Brett poked his ID into the crack and said, "I'm sorry to trouble you at this time of night but it's the police. We need to ask you a few questions."

"Police!" the voice retorted. "Are you sure?"

Brett and Clare exchanged a wry grin. "Yes, we're sure," Brett replied. "Detective Inspector Lawless and Detective Sergeant Tilley."

With a groan, Harry closed the door while he released the security chain. Then he opened the door again and muttered, "You'd better come in, I suppose, before I catch my death of cold."

To Brett and Clare it didn't seem cold at all but they slipped inside quickly anyway. Both of them had already dismissed the idea that Harry could be responsible for abducting anyone. He was frail, arthritic and more concerned about defending himself from crime than committing it. He probably lost things because he was slow and easily distracted, worrying about how he was going to afford his electricity, rates, medicines, water and gas. He would not cope with a bouncy seven-year-old girl in his quiet, shabby home, which smelled of old age.

Assuming that Mr Hobson's hearing was not what it used to be, Brett asked loudly, "We need to know if you bought a couple of packets of Zantac from Waters Pharmacy today."

"Young man, I may suffer from a hundred and one aches and pains but my ears are in perfect working order. No need to shout."

"Sorry," Brett said as Clare tried not to smirk. "*Did* you buy any Zantac today?"

"Never heard of it," Harry answered. "What is it?"

"They're pills for ulcers."

"Oh, those," Harry replied. "Yes. I go to the chemist on the corner for something for my ulcers. They give me something. I don't worry about what they're called."

"And did you lose a packet of them?"

"Oh, damn nuisance, those pavements."

"Sorry?" Brett queried with a frown.

"I think I lost 'em when I tripped over a paving slab, near the wood."

"When was this?"

Harry shrugged. "This evening, I suppose. Playing me up, the ulcers were. Did you really say your name was Lawless?"

Brett nodded. "Yes."

The old man cackled happily. "Detective called Lawless. That's a good 'un."

To help her partner out, Clare interjected, "I hope you weren't hurt when you fell over. Did you see anything unusual near the wood?"

"They didn't make policemen like you in my day," he said. Then he added, "Anyway, have you found my pills? Is that what this is all about?"

Clare did her best to smile. Harry was living in some long-gone era when police officers were always male and detectives might be sent out to return some tablets to their rightful owner. "No," she replied. "We've found your pills, yes, but our questions have got to do with something else. Something very important. The kidnapping of a little girl."

"That's cruel, that is," he said with a grimace.

"Quite a coincidence as well. I saw a little girl today. Now, where was it?"

Clare waited patiently but nothing came.

Brett took a photograph of Kerry from his pocket and showed it to Harry. "Is that the girl you saw, by any chance?"

Harry squinted at the photo and muttered, "I can't see that. Too small. Just a minute." From a sideboard he plucked some reading spectacles and then peered at the photograph again. "Yes. That could well be the lass."

"This is very important," Brett stressed. "Where did you see her?"

"Was it near the place you lost the pills?" Clare added, trying to jog his memory.

Harry wagged his forefinger in Clare's direction. "You know, you've got it. No wonder they made you a policeman."

"Police *officer*," Clare said, hoping to get his attention off her gender and back on to Kerry as quickly as possible. Brett had become frustrated with Harry's constant drifting and left the rest of the interview to Clare. "You saw her near the wood, then?" she prompted.

"That'd be it," Harry answered. "She was the one who helped me up and gathered all my stuff. Well," he added, "maybe not all. She must have missed those Zanussi pills. Still, I can't blame her. She was only trying to help."

"After she picked up your shopping, what

happened?" Clare enquired eagerly.

"I came home," Harry announced unhelpfully.

"Remember, this girl who helped you has been taken away. Her parents are desperate," said Clare, trying to appeal to his sympathy. "You might have seen something."

"I didn't hear about it on the news."

"No," Clare replied with infinite composure while Brett paced up and down like a restless lion. "This won't get on the telly. It could be dangerous if there's any publicity."

"Hush-hush operation," Harry mumbled quietly as if he'd been caught up in international espionage. "Did they take her dog?"

"No. Her dog's back home, where *she* should be. After you left her, did you look back? You say your hearing's good. Did you hear anything?"

"Heard her dog. She'd tied him to a post. Barking, he was. Then the girl shouted and he stopped. He growled instead. Growled a lot. Vicious thing. That's all I heard."

"What did she shout?"

Mr Hobson shrugged. "Couldn't tell. I reckoned she'd be telling her dog to stop his barking."

"Is that all? Did you hear or see a car, for example?"

"I'm not sure." He fiddled with the glasses in his hand, yawned and then said, "Now you mention it, yes, a car door slammed. Twice, I think. Do you two work all through the night? I suppose, at your age, you're up to that sort of thing. I'm normally fast asleep by now."

"We won't keep you much longer," Clare said. "Did you *see* the car?"

"Now, that's a difficult one," he said as he stared at the ceiling.

His glasses slipped from his hand and threatened to fall down the gap in his chair, where they could be lost for days or weeks. While Harry thought about her query, Clare rescued the spectacles and returned them to the sideboard. Harry didn't even notice.

Abruptly, he gave his verdict. "Yes." He nodded and gazed triumphantly towards Clare. "I'm pretty sure I did."

"Good." Starting with the easy question, she asked, "What colour was it?"

Harry looked suddenly confident. "White," he stated. Then he frowned, thought about it a bit more and added, "Or was that the car outside the chemist? Perhaps it was. I think the one that came out of the wood was blue. Could've been blue, or maybe green."

It could have been a small car or a lorry. Harry couldn't be precise. He was equally vague about the driver. According to Harry, the driver was either a man or a woman, dressed in grey or some other colour, and was wearing a hat – or not.

Clare and Brett thanked him and left. At least they had got a better picture of the events at the edge of the wood, even if they didn't have any firm details.

* * *

Brett knew that Phil and Chloe would not have gone to bed. He went back to update them. Near the house, he linked arms with Clare again so they looked like a normal couple. Just in case. By the light that still blazed from the living-room window, Clare looked at her partner and observed, "You're upset."

Brett halted. He confessed quietly, "I've got a bad feeling about this one, Clare."

Trying to put him in a better frame of mind, she said, "You scientific blokes don't get bad feelings. You just get evidence."

"There's something I haven't told you," Brett whispered.

"Oh?"

"I'm her godfather." Brett gazed into Clare's face and then continued, "That means if anything happens to her parents, I'm responsible for her. Right now, I'd say they're as good as out of it so, in a sense, something *has* happened to them."

Clare nodded slowly. "Godfather," she murmured. "That's why you had a photo of her."

"That's why I've got a bad feeling. The detective in me wants the evidence. The godfather in me is getting the bad feeling."

"I'm sorry, Brett," she said, squeezing his arm. "Come on. Let's get on with it. You'll feel better if we're *doing* something, making progress."

Brett nodded. If he was going to crack this case, he knew he'd need Clare to drag him through it. He thought of her as an equal partner despite the difference in their ranks. He wished that she had been promoted after her part in the Messenger case, but the all-male board had decided against. It was probably a clear case of sex discrimination. If she had been a man, she might have been considered more seriously as promotion material. Brett realized that Clare felt snubbed, but she did not resent his own appointment as full detective inspector. Even so, he had been more comfortable with her when he'd been a probationary DI. Then, as a detective sergeant, Clare still had a claim to equality. Her established position balanced his higher but unconfirmed rank. With the selection board's decisions, that balance had been dashed.

Inside, Brett made four mugs of strong coffee and gave the Chapmans the latest news. He also exonerated Copper. Brett had been convinced by Harry Hobson's account that Copper had freed himself from the spot where Kerry had left him and set upon the kidnapper. "We've got a witness who says he saw a dog tied to a fence post. Judging by the state of the post now, it seems he tugged heroically to get free and help Kerry. At one point, he stopped barking and turned to growling, we're told. I bet he barked while he was still tied up but, when he got free, he started growling and had a go at whoever was in the wood. Unfortunately, all he got was a bit of coat, or whatever that material's from. But he did his bit, I think."

Phil laid his hand on Copper's neck. "Pity you

couldn't..." Phil sighed and stopped talking to the red setter.

Chloe was even more anxious. "What do you think they'll do to her, Brett?" she whimpered.

Brett shook his head. "I don't know. Probably nothing. Just use her to bargain for whatever they want. They won't harm her while she's useful to them."

"I'm scared," Chloe said. "I wish they'd taken me rather than Kerry. I could've coped with that."

"Once we've got the results from the wood, Chloe, we'll be in a better position to figure it out." Trying to be less morbid, Brett enquired, "Any phone calls?"

Phil was exhausted and haggard. He shook his head. "But one of your men has doctored the phone. He's upstairs, keeping watch."

In the darkened front bedroom, Adam from the surveillance unit had set up his den, surrounded by a video, fancy electronic gadgets, and a DAT recorder. He put down his binoculars and greeted Brett and Clare.

"Anything?" Brett enquired.

"No," Adam answered. "I'm as sure as I can be that no one's watching the house."

"And how sure's that?"

"Pretty sure. But just in case..." He nodded towards the video camera, mounted on a tripod and peeping over the windowsill like a vigilant snoop. "Just to check it's working, I've got some lovely footage of you two snuggling up to each other on the path. Very touching," he said with a laugh. "Back at HQ, the lads'll love it!" He glanced at Clare and added, "Sorry. Lads *and* lasses."

"No, I think you were right first time," Clare retorted. "Only lads would be interested in that."

Brett was not in the mood for banter, and he knew that, following the selection board's rejection of Clare's application for promotion, she would be irritated by gibes about gender. "Let's go," he said to her. "We're breaking Adam's concentration." At the door, Brett turned and said, "This one's important to me. Don't miss anything. I want to know if there's the slightest whiff of someone watching the house or a phone call. And Phil thinks he's been stalked so keep your eyes open for her."

"A stalker? A female one? I thought stalking was a male preserve."

"No," Clare interjected. "Men don't have a monopoly on stalking. Women can do it as well. I'm sure it's just as rotten for the victim either way."

Before they left the Chapmans, they assured Chloe that there was no sign that the house was under observation. Even so, Brett and Clare walked away with a friendly, sympathetic wave, looking as little like police officers as possible.

It was unfortunate for Louise Jenson that, when she stumbled across her first major inquiry during her foundation course, it involved the country's most notorious serial killer. An unpleasant and disturbing debut. After witnessing the Messenger's handiwork close up, having felt his arm crushing her throat, she needed a change, for the sake of her own sanity. She'd got too close to him and her nerves had taken a hammering. Still in her probationary period, she had asked to be transferred across the border from Nottinghamshire Constabulary into the South Yorkshire Police force. On compassionate grounds, and because John Macfarlane, Brett and her own tutor sergeant in Nottinghamshire had given her glowing references, the posting had gone ahead. What Louise lacked in confidence she counter-balanced with dedication, initiative and hard work. When Brett asked for a junior officer to check surgeries and hospitals for victims of dog bites, he requested Louise. He got his own way. As part of her training, Louise was given an attachment to DI Lawless's investigation.

Back at the police station, going into the office that would become his incident room in the morning, Brett was taken aback. It was almost midnight and Louise was still working on her report. Brett looked at his watch and said, "Now that's what I call keen."

"Nearly done, sir," Louise said rather stiffly.

Brett smiled and sat down opposite her. "Louise, if you're going to work with us, there's one rule you should never break."

Timidly, Louise asked, "Oh? What's that?"

"My name's Brett and Clare's is Clare. None of this sir and ma'am bit, OK? Save it for the chief."

"The sir, that is," Clare chipped in. "Not the ma'am."

"All right," Louise replied, with a tentative smile. "My report's almost finished. But I'm not very good at spelling. Teachers never could drill it into me, you know. After *c*, does *i* come before *e*, or is it the other way round?" Her cheeks reddened.

"The other way round, but I'll know what you mean either way," Brett said genially. "But tell me, have you had any luck?"

Louise nodded. "Two dog bites so far, but it was too late to get in touch with every surgery. I'll do the rest first thing in the morning."

"Good. What about the two you did trace?"

"I don't think they're what you want. One was a twelve-year-old lad who teased a dog a bit too much. The other was a chap living out Hillsborough way. Badly mauled arm. He told the hospital it was an unprovoked attack but he wouldn't tell them where. The nurse was suspicious about him. I took the liberty of looking him up on file. He's a burglar, you know, a career burglar. In and out of here every few months. So I crosschecked against burglaries reported today and found one in Walkley where the owner disturbed the burglar and his dog had a good go at him. I've e-mailed the investigating officer and forensic is matching blood stains at the scene against this burglar's file. I think that might clear it up."

Despite his sombre mood, Brett grinned. "No wonder you're here late. You've been solving the whole city's crime as well as working for me. Carry on. I'll even forgive your lousy spelling if you keep that up."

Before he left, Brett despatched an electronic copy of Kerry's picture and her description to all forces. In his request for any sightings, he classified the photograph as confidential. It was not to be released to the press nor shown to the public.

Brett slept fitfully. His brain was too active. Instead of sleeping, he was wondering how to track down a stalker and interview three vehicle engineers without disclosing that he was a police officer. He wished that the kidnapper's note had not forced him to promise Phil and Chloe that he would not reveal that he was investigating the abduction. He could not risk questioning Ross Mundee, Hilary Garner or Alan Fox properly. If one of them was holding Kerry to ransom in the hope of exchanging her for Phil's industrial secrets, Brett could jeopardize her safety by revealing his identity.

By morning, though, he had a plan.

In Brett's kitchen, the Magic Eye picture that Clare had given him at Christmas no longer decorated his fridge door. He'd removed it after concluding the Messenger case because it reminded him too much of the struggle to discern a pattern in the killer's nation-wide trail of sickening murders. Brett had struggled to see the laughing clown in the Magic Eye image, and its absurd grin had finally seemed grotesque to him. Clare understood at once why he'd thrown out her gift. It was important for the mental health of any police officer to ditch as much baggage as possible from such a distressing case. Both of them had to look forward and not back into the Messenger's ugly mire.

For the first time in months, Brett did not jog around the park before showering and taking breakfast. He was too preoccupied. He bolted down some cereal, drank a large mug of coffee, then left for work. A quick call to Adam's mobile phone confirmed that everything had remained quiet at the Chapmans' house. "No great surprise," Adam announced dispassionately. "It's quite usual to make the relatives sweat a bit first." Lowering his voice, he added, "And these two are certainly sweating."

"Anyone watching the house?"

"There's only one twitching curtain here and that's the one I'm behind," Adam said. "No one's keeping watch, I'm certain. You don't have to come and go on tiptoe."

Brett called Sabre Cars and asked for Ross Mundee. The engineer himself had not arrived at work but his answering machine promised that he would respond to any message. Brett said, "Hello. This is Brett Richardson. I'm a science writer working on a piece about environmentally friendly vehicles. I'm contacting all the major players in the business in the hope of getting brief interviews on progress. I was told you'd be an ideal man to talk to. It won't take long. I'm in your area today and I'd really appreciate a few words." He dictated his mobile phone number and rang off. He decided not to use his real name in case Mundee was the kidnapper and decided to research Brett's background. Equipped with his actual surname, Mundee would easily uncover his true identity as a police officer.

Soon after, Clare turned up and together they drove through the heavy heat haze to the forensic laboratories to see Greta. Approaching her, Brett put up his hands in mock surrender. "I know," he said. "It's too early. You haven't got much yet. But what have you got?"

Greta was holding a gun and a glove – both sealed inside separate polythene bags – that had just come in from a different case. She put them down and declared, "You're right. It's too soon." As quickly as she could, she logged the new arrivals into the laboratory information-management system, then turned to Brett and Clare. "There's some progress, though. That fence post had Copper's fur attached to it. When he moved away, a nick in the post pulled out a good few hairs."

"That tallies with what an eyewitness said. So, as we thought, it was Copper who yanked on the post and pulled it over. Any sure evidence that he attacked whoever abducted Kerry and grabbed a mouthful of coat?"

Greta nodded. "*Some* evidence. We haven't matched the teeth-marks on that bit of material yet, but there was a red-setter hair attached to it. That's a start. We're still looking for any other traces: soil, fibres, saliva, that sort of thing. And the fabric itself. We used infrared spectroscopy. It's mainly polyester. About seventy-five per cent. The rest is split pretty evenly between viscose and cotton. We haven't identified what it's from yet, but I don't think it's particularly special, unfortunately. Probably high-street store stuff."

"Let me know if there's any developments," Brett requested.

"Sure," Greta replied. "Before you go, though, we've got ESDA on the notepaper. You'll be interested. On the page above the kidnap note, someone wrote some sort of code number."

Brett was intrigued. "What was it?"

Greta handed him a photograph of the ESDA result. The letters and numbers were not fully defined, but they were clear enough.

EOT 01203775

Brett glanced at Greta and asked, "Any ideas?"

The forensic scientist shrugged. "I just find the evidence. It's your job to make sense of it."

Clare suggested, "Let's give it to Louise. See if she can come up with anything."

"There's something else," Greta added. "Distinctly less interesting, I'm afraid. That bit of cotton you found on a bramble further into the wood. The blood group matches Kerry's. Not a huge step forward. May not even be significant. Possibly no more than a thumb pricked on the bramble. Which reminds me. There's something we *didn't* find at the kidnap scene. No more of Kerry's blood, you'll be pleased to know. No one else's blood, either. That's it for now. I'm waiting for mass spectrometry on the residue from the syringe. There wasn't enough for any other method."

"Thanks, Greta. Keep up the good work. I'm still putting my money on the material and the syringe.

Give me a call or e-mail Louise Jenson, will you, when you squeeze the juice out of them?"

"You got it."

Chloe had always looked immaculate. But not now. She was worn by worry. Phil was in need of some sleep, a shave and a shower. Adam had been right. The tension was taking its toll on them. Chloe exclaimed, "You look like cops! You didn't let anyone see you coming here, did you?"

Brett grasped her arm and said gently, "No one's watching the house, Chloe. We know they're not. It's OK."

That morning, Brett had not put his arm round Clare as they approached the Chapmans' house. He was pleased not to have to endure the embarrassment, but he had also felt deprived of an excuse to show his affection for Clare. Before, he'd held her to protect Kerry. That's what he told himself. That's why Clare had agreed to it. It was a duty, not a choice. Clare was his partner while on duty and friend when off duty. There was respect and fondness, Brett believed, but there was also a line that they wouldn't – and shouldn't – cross. Brett imagined that Clare, after once posing as his girlfriend, was not now giving it any further thought or regretting its passing.

"Any news?" Phil prompted before even greeting his friend.

"Not a lot," Brett confessed.

"Why haven't we heard anything? Just that note," Chloe cried, grasping one hand nervously in the other.

"Because they want you to stew a bit, I'm afraid," Brett answered ruefully, trying to keep his own anxiety concealed. "Just like the message said. They want you to feel incomplete for a while. I'm sorry. But we've got some leads. Whoever wrote the note might have scribbled down a code number of some sort on the page above. Does EOT 01203775 mean anything to you?"

Chloe shook her head helplessly and turned to Phil, yearning for him to cast some light on it.

Phil shrugged. "Not really. A telephone number? A car-engine identification number? Or a chassis number?"

"Interesting idea," Brett murmured. If the number was an ID code for a car, it would suggest that the writer *was* in the car trade. Exactly what Phil had proposed. "I want to go and see Ross Mundee," Brett said. Before Phil and Chloe could voice their objections, he explained, "I'm going as a journalist, doing a story on exhaust pollution."

Phil looked dubious. "You'll still look like a policeman."

"Oh, I think I can—"

At the sudden sound of the door bell, Brett and Clare sprang into action without a word, like a well-rehearsed team. Clare flew out of the back door and began to creep round to the front. Brett stood behind the door, flattened against the wall, while Phil walked hesitantly towards it. At the end of the hall, Chloe waited, biting her nails, and Copper barked.

The sudden stress was relieved by Adam's voice from the top of the stairs. "It's a young girl."

When Phil opened the door, a small girl in a bright green dress was standing there. Much to the visitor's surprise, Chloe dashed up to her and exclaimed, "Farida! Have you seen Kerry?"

Farida looked blank. "I just came to see if she's coming out to play." She glanced round as Clare appeared suddenly behind her. Frightened, she turned her head to gaze at Chloe and ask, "What's going on, Mrs Chapman?"

"You'd better come in for a bit," said Phil.

While they broke the news to Farida that Kerry had been taken from the wood yesterday, Farida stared at Phil in shock. "Yesterday?" she spluttered. "That's when Makbool said he saw her."

Immediately Brett repeated, "Makbool?"

"My brother."

Clare asked, "Where did he see her? In the wood?"

Farida nodded nervously.

"Do you know where exactly?"

"No."

Clare knelt by Farida and said, "Can you take us to Makbool now? It's very important to Kerry. Is he at home?"

"He's playing computer games with Liam."

"Are your mum and dad in as well?" Brett asked.

He could only conduct an interview in the presence of a parent.

"Mum's at work but Dad's home." Farida hesitated, then asked fearfully, "Kerry is going to be all right, isn't she?"

It was Clare who answered. "Yes, of course she is. We're doing everything we can to get her back. And Makbool might be able to help us get her back quicker."

Copper jumped up and the door bell chimed again. Brett and Clare were about to go through their paces once more when Adam shouted, "I think it's your artist, Brett."

While the artist worked with Phil to develop a sketch of his stalker, Brett and Clare went down the road to Farida's house. At first, Makbool and Liam were annoyed to have their game interrupted, then they became coy, and finally they loosened up with Clare. They had more to say about a dead rat than about Kerry and unfortunately their story added nothing extra to the inquiry. If they had bumped into her later, they might have had more to tell. Their presence might even have thwarted the kidnap.

As Brett left Makbool's house, Ross Mundee called and agreed to grant Brett a few minutes of his precious time that same Tuesday morning. Clearly, Sabre was eager for publicity.

Back in the incident room Louise remarked, "That ESDA scribble. If it's a telephone number, it's

Coventry's area code – 01203. But it can't be all there, you know. We've only got 775 left."

"Mmm." Brett thought about it for a moment and then said, "Check it against the number for a company called Ventura in Coventry, and the home number of someone called Hilary Garner. Then," he added, "get on to vehicle manufacturers, car-hire companies, the car-theft brigade and the police national computer. See if it might be an engine ID or chassis number, or any other car identification. And keep your fingers crossed it's a reference to the get-away car." Brett paused before continuing, "Try the banks as well. See if it's a bank-account number. I think you'll find they're eight digits."

While she listened, Louise cocked her head to one side. The habit gave her the bearing of an attentive, curious and bashful bird approaching an offered titbit. "OK," she said deferentially.

Clare said, "While you're impersonating a journalist at Sabre Cars, Brett, I'll make some general inquiries at Hallam Golf Club. Kerry must have walked right past it. Let me have a copy of Kerry's picture to jog memories. And I'll get a list of everyone playing yesterday evening."

At Sabre, Brett was taken to a small conference room to meet Ross Mundee. The vehicle engineer was a short, thin and fidgety man in rimless glasses. His face was pinched, full of hard edges. When the two men shook hands, Brett hardly noticed the pressure of Mundee's limp grip, despite the prominence of his bones. The contact lacked all warmth and signified only Mundee's impatience to complete the interview. The engineer might court publicity but clearly he resented the time that it took. Brett sat down and muttered, "I hope you don't mind." He indicated the cassette recorder that he'd borrowed from surveillance. Just as Clark Kent disguised himself flimsily with spectacles, Brett used a tape recorder. Neither ploy was convincing. Both Superman and a policeman made implausible newspaper reporters.

"No, I don't mind," Ross Mundee replied. He lit up a cigarette and pulled an ashtray towards himself.

Turning on the machine, Brett promised, "I won't keep you long anyway. I want to ask you the usual question about petrol versus cleaner fuels and then move on quickly to some specific points."

"Which journal are you working for?" Ross probed.

Recalling his days reading chemistry at university, Brett answered without hesitation, "*Chemistry and Industry*. The article'll come out towards the end of the year." Before Mundee could ask any more awkward questions, Brett started the mock interview with a provocative question. "In these days of concern about the environment and global warming, does the car have a future?"

Like a true politician of vehicle manufacturing, Ross answered, "Certainly it's got a future. The right to travel is a freedom that the public won't give up. *If* there's an environment problem, technology has to change to prevent it. You can't take away the freedom."

"And is Sabre trying to meet that challenge?"

"We've been at the forefront of catalytic–converter technology."

Brett interrupted, saying, "That takes care of some pollution problems but what about reducing or eliminating carbon–dioxide emissions?"

"To do that realistically, you'd have to change the fuel," Ross replied. He took a drag on his cigarette and let out a stream of grey smoke.

Brett was surprised that a man working towards a cleaner environment was prepared to pollute his own lungs so heavily. Wishing that he was not bound by the pretence of being a journalist, Brett queried, "Are *you* investigating the alternatives? Natural gas, biodiesel, alcohol, hydrogen?"

Ross Mundee stared penetratingly at Brett for a second before responding. "The only one of those that doesn't create carbon dioxide when it's burnt is hydrogen."

Brett nodded. "Do you have an interest in hydrogen as a fuel? Are you developing a prototype engine?" This was the heart of Brett's interrogation. If Ross expected to acquire Phil's secrets on the hydrogen car by bargaining with Kerry, he would have to say that he was involved in the necessary research. Otherwise, when he produced a hydrogen–fuelled car all of a sudden, everyone would ponder where the technology had come from. It would be obvious that Ross Mundee was guilty of kidnapping and cheating. But if he pretended that he was already working in the area, he might be tripped up by Brett's next question into his strategy and progress.

Cagily, the engineer replied, "I think we can expect developments towards that goal quite soon."

"Are you thinking of your own work or a competitor's?"

"I'd be surprised if Sabre were alone in investigating hydrogen as a vehicle and aviation fuel," Ross answered.

"Would your approach be on-board generation of hydrogen or on-board storage?"

"I can't be specific about our methods," Ross said tersely.

Either he was genuinely protecting his own research or he was hiding the fact that he didn't yet know what Phil's invention was. "Who are your competitors?" asked Brett, trying to look innocent.

"I am not interested in other manufacturers," Mundee said.

Brett knew that he *had* taken an interest in Phil. Mundee had tried to recruit Phil to Sabre. Virtually threatened him, according to Phil. As a science reporter, though, Brett could not probe this fiction. Frustrated, Brett turned off the cassette and thanked Ross for his co-operation. "Oh," he added, feigning an afterthought. "Can you write down your title and full name so I get it right in my article?" He pushed a piece of paper towards Mundee.

Ross declined the request. He balanced the remains of his cigarette on the lip of the ashtray and took a business card from his pocket. With his left hand, he flicked the small card brusquely across the table. "It's all on there," he remarked.

"Ah. Thanks," Brett replied. He pocketed the card, silently cursing his luck. Ross Mundee had avoided supplying him with a sample of his hand-writing and ink.

Almost as soon as Brett had made himself com-fortable in his car, Louise called him on his mobile phone. She sounded panic-striken.

"Brett, I think you'd better get out to Attercliffe. Princess Street near the railway station. We've got a derailed train."

"Louise," Brett interrupted, "I've got enough on my plate without—"

"Sorry, but the wagons fell down an embankment on to an arch workshop below. Word's come in that there's evidence of a little girl—"

"I'm on my way," Brett replied. Before he put his foot down, to engage in battle with Sheffield's congested traffic and dodge the trams, he added, "Get Clare on the job as well. Tell her I'll meet her there."

It looked like something from a disaster movie. A scene of devastation after a bomb blast. But this was not a carefully controlled film set. It was real chaos. A truck had demolished the brick wall of the arches and taken a nosedive down the embankment. It had crunched a parked lorry that, ironically, was inscribed with the words *Demolition and Excavation Service*. Now the railway wagon was balanced precariously on its end. In the brilliant daylight it cast a shadow like the giant pointer of a sundial. The rest of the goods train was perched at an ominous angle up above, on the embankment. Electric cables hung down from the churned-up trackside. Below, splintered joists and door panels jutted out from the battered workshop like horribly broken bones. Rubble was scattered everywhere. A stationary car, waiting for the automobile valeting service in the next archway, had been crushed by falling masonry and ballast spilled from the wagon.

Princess Street was in the middle of Sheffield's industrial maze. It was a narrow road, with the railway on one side, and an electroplating factory and pewter manufacturer on the other. The neglected workshop was sandwiched between a plant-hire company and a car-cleaning business, staffed by students in their vacation. Diggers, work huts, tyres, tarpaulins and metal drums littered the place. The dogs that guarded the plant hire premises had been moved away and were barking almost continuously from a safe distance. Police had cordoned off the danger area and firefighters were bringing in specialized equipment and cranes.

At the edge of the danger zone, the uniformed police officer in charge was talking to the chief firefighter. Interrupting them, Brett flashed his warrant card. "Heard you got a sighting of a girl in there." With his hand on his forehead, shielding his eyes from the sunlight, he gazed at the wreckage and shuddered inwardly. He wasn't sure how anyone in the dilapidated workshop under the arches could have survived.

"Not a sighting when the train derailed," the policeman replied. "Behind the truck there's a disused bike shop. Well, there was. Sold second-hand mountain and racing bikes. Nicked. We bust the operation a few weeks ago. It's been deserted since then. But a witness in one of the electroplating units across the road says he saw a youngster – almost certainly a girl – and an adult knocking around in there last night. He saw the adult again early this morning – too far into the arches to judge sex and age – but he doesn't remember seeing either of them come out."

Brett prayed that no one had been caught in the accident. Especially not Kerry. But he had to check. "What was the girl wearing?" he enquired.

"He couldn't say. It was too dark. And it was only a glimpse through a dirty window. The best he came up with is casual." The officer, sweltering inside his uniform, wiped his moist brow. "He was only at the window for a second or two. They could easily have come out unseen before the train derailed."

"And they might not have done." Brett turned to the firefighter and said, "I'm going in there."

The chief laughed sardonically. "You've got to be joking! I don't care who you are. You're not going in."

"There could be a kidnapped girl in the ruins."

"Well, you can't go in till my team's made it safe. The gas and electricity supplies to the district are off and we've stopped all trains, but that wagon," he said, nodding towards the balanced truck, "could fall at any moment. And so could more of the brickwork. If there *is* a girl in there, I'm keeping it down to one casualty. I haven't even given my team the go-ahead yet."

"Can't you get a robotic camera in?" Brett asked.

"Too much rubble for its wheels to negotiate. We're waiting for hand-held heat-seeking cameras and specially trained dogs."

Brett strode back to his car and called Clare, asking her to pick up Copper on her way. Then he paced up and down, getting increasingly frustrated by the delay.

Brett was delving into the boot of his car when Clare screeched to a halt. She joined him and briefly, he explained the situation to her.

Holding the red setter by his leash, she queried, "If it's too dangerous to do a search, why do you want Copper and why are you getting a torch out?" Of course, she knew the answer.

"Because I owe Phil and Chloe. Because I owe Kerry. She's virtually a relative. I'm going in to have a look around. I'm hoping Copper will be able to nose her out if she's in there."

"Hang on a second," Clare said. "I'll get my torch as well."

Brett peered at his partner. "No, Clare. This is *my* job. There's no point risking both of us."

"That's more chivalry than sense," she retorted. "What about shifting heavy stuff? You'll need help. And if you have to use both hands for something, how are you going to hold a torch? Besides," she added, "haven't you seen the *X Files*? In the dingy building scene there's always two torches."

Brett smiled. He was grateful. Grateful that she

was willing to help, grateful that she could banish the tension. "You've been reading the police training manual again: *X Files* section on entry and search without consent or warrant."

"That's right," Clare joked. "Just follow me and you'll be all right. I've seen exactly how it's done on the box."

"You didn't take the dog-handling course as well, did you?"

"Sorry."

Brett knelt down by the bewildered red setter and stroked him for a few seconds. Then he said, "Can you help us? I bet you can. Where's Kerry? Find Kerry, Copper."

Immediately, the dog became alert and smelled the air.

"Come on," Brett encouraged him. "Over here." Ignoring the shouts of warning from two of the emergency workers, Brett picked his way through the debris and round a skip that was overflowing with junk. Copper seemed to know what was expected of him and he sniffed along the rubble and the fallen bricks for any trace of Kerry.

The upended truck creaked ominously like a drunk groaning just before falling to the ground. Leading the way, Brett gave it a wide berth in case it decided to topple into a more stable position and crush the three of them. Once behind it, they were plunged into a darkness like sudden nightfall. Daylight failed to penetrate the workshop. Both Brett and Clare shivered with the abrupt cold and damp. They turned on their torches and the beams leapt eerily from their hands, producing two columns of bright light and a diffuse glow in the empty workplace. Like crazy disconnected headlamps, the torches probed the gloom. Ducking under a joist that had splintered like a matchstick and now hung down from the archway, Brett and Clare stepped warily inside. The canopy consisted of curved brickwork, claustrophobic and alarmingly cracked. Between the bricks, the mortar was uneven and discoloured. The beams picked out glistening green patches where algae were growing in damp crevices. In places, falling dust glinted in the torchlight, a warning of serious collapses yet to come. The three walls were bare, dirty and desolate. On the right, a wooden panel separated the main workshop area from an inner room, a cabin or a closet. The concrete floor was littered with rubbish. Newspapers, tattered bike saddles, a torn calendar featuring cycles, used batteries, three bald bike tyres and some warped wheels, and a spent puncture-repair kit with several exhausted tubes of rubber solution. Clare's spotlight lingered momentarily on something that sparkled and reflected the beam. Squatting by it, she found only an abandoned spanner.

Outside, there was a rumble and a loud thud as another large clump of bricks fell from the embankment on to the concrete court. Brett and Clare ignored the fearsome noise but for an instant, they both considered what might have happened if they'd been outside.

Somewhere in the roof, bricks grated against each other as they shifted treacherously. More particles of mortar drifted down from the fault line. Both Brett and Clare felt vulnerable. Their grip on their lives had become flimsy. At any moment, the ceiling could cave in and bury them alive.

Copper sniffed the floor and looked up at Brett. It wasn't a vacant expression. It was indecisive. Copper might have detected something. "What is it?" Brett whispered. "Kerry?" Copper put his nose back on the ground and meandered through the workshop. Then, detecting a definite scent, he began to guide Brett purposefully towards the door into the cubicle on the right. "Over here," Brett murmured to Clare. His voice echoed round the artificial cavern and Copper's determined pawing at the wooden panel sounded like unearthly tapping on a coffin.

"Probably an office of sorts," Clare suggested.

Brett yanked on the handle: the door rattled but would not budge. He banged on the door and shouted, "Kerry!" The noise boomed throughout the vault.

After a few silent moments, Clare said, "Well, the dog's telling us to take a look inside, so why hang about? Let me do the honours." She took a deep breath and then struck out with her foot, connecting with the door near its handle. There was a loud crack. The wood splintered around the lock and the door flew back.

Immediately Copper barked enthusiastically, then tugged Brett into the cobwebby crypt and started to whine. The dog's reaction confirmed beyond doubt that Kerry had been inside the dismal office. But now the place was deserted. The spotlights shone on a rickety desk, a tool box, more discarded paper, and a small metal cabinet. On the floor was a piece of rope. Abandoned rubbish. Nothing alive.

Brett sighed. "This is—"

Clare completed his sentence. "Awful. No one would want to be locked in here."

"She must have been scared silly." Brett inhaled, shook his head and then said, "Let's not disturb it. As soon as it's made safe, we'll get forensics in to do a proper search."

"Just a temporary holding station for her, presumably." Clare touched her partner's arm. "Look on the bright side, Brett. At least she wasn't here to get hurt when the train derailed. And she didn't have to stay in this awful place for too long."

"Yeah, but where is she now? Somewhere even worse?"

"Come on," Clare said. "We've done all we can. We can't do any more without messing it up for forensics. Let's get clear before the ceiling comes down."

"OK." Reluctantly, Brett turned his back on the grimy office and dragged the disappointed dog away. Brett wished that he was carrying Kerry out of the industrial desert and back to her parents. His success at locating her first hiding place was too limited to satisfy him.

Before setting foot outside, Brett and Clare turned off their torches and glanced upwards as if expecting deadly rain. Their eyes narrowed against the brilliance. They were eager to step into the light and warmth of the summer day that the damp arch had obliterated but they were aware that it posed a considerable danger. The wagon was tilting even more sharply now. It looked like a cruel, heavy giant, waiting to embrace and devour its victim. Stones and small pieces of mortar cascaded down the wall like a mini-landslide. When and where would the next major fall come?

Brett shrugged and said, "Let's just go and hope for the best. Skirt round the truck, though. We wouldn't stand a chance if it fell."

It was like walking through a world made unstable by a constant, rumbling earthquake. Out in the sunshine, Brett could see that Copper and Clare had acquired a layer of dust and dirt. He assumed that he must look the same: prematurely grey. Behind them, a length of piping fell and, when it hit the piles of bricks below, it let out chaotic chimes until it came to rest. Brett staggered and muttered, "Ow!" as the loose bricks under his feet moved, tipping him forward and twisting his ankle. He was agile enough to avoid tumbling but he halted while he checked out his foot. Just then, a huge and heavy chunk of the embankment shifted and began to topple. "Go!" Clare shouted.

No longer picking their route carefully, they dashed across the carnage of the concrete yard as the bricks crashed thunderously to the ground and lay in a shroud of dust. Fortunately, Brett, Clare and Copper had put enough distance between themselves and the fall to be safe. If they had lingered for twenty seconds more, they would not have got out alive.

The chief firefighter was livid. "You could've been killed!" he yelled so loudly that he might have caused another avalanche. "Luckily all you've got is an entry in my report. You haven't heard the last of this. No wonder they call you Lawless."

Brett replied, "You write your report as you see fit but, before that, make this place safe as soon as you can, will you? A seven-year-old girl *was* held inside. I'm certain. But she's not there now. If we're going to save her, we need all the evidence we can get. We need a forensic team in there pronto." He gave his mobile-phone number to the firefighter and limped away. Then he and Clare went to tell Phil and Chloe the latest news and to return Copper. He did not give his ankle injury another thought and had soon walked off the pain.

After a wash and brush-up, they drove to the Chapmans' house, where Brett tried to put on a brave face. "I'm sure Kerry was there, because of Copper," he told his friends. "We nearly got her."

"But you didn't," Chloe whispered as she wept.

Taking Clare's advice to look on the bright side,

Brett said, "At least she wasn't hurt in the accident. And two really good things have come out of it. We'll get another batch of forensic results. There's always clues to be found. And we can go about a normal police investigation from now on. It's out in the open. See what I mean? Police attending the derailing get a whiff of a girl being held. The description given by a witness leads to Kerry. We end up at your door. You've got nothing to do with involving the police. A crashed train puts us on to it, not you."

Phil and Chloe looked uneasy but they admitted that there was a logic to Brett's words.

"It makes things a lot easier for us," Brett proclaimed, trying to put fresh heart into them. "And a lot better for Kerry." He still felt like a clown whose tired act was turning sour in front of a cynical audience. Phil and Chloe wanted their daughter, not a light at the end of a long tunnel.

Clare recounted her conversation with a golfer who had seen Kerry and a red setter yesterday – just before the kidnap. The player was concentrating on his game so he didn't take much notice and anyway, he wouldn't have been able to see a vehicle parked at the edge of the wood from the golf course. Clare's lead had come to nothing.

"What now then?" Phil queried.

"House-to-house inquiries in case a neighbour saw who delivered that note," Brett said. "Show that sketch of your stalker around. I want to know who she was, and why she's stopped pestering you all of a sudden. And proper interviews with Hilary Garner and Alan Fox. As well as following up the forensic data from the wood and Princess Street. And we've got a good police officer working behind the scenes on bits and pieces, like that code number. We're not short of leads."

Brett glanced at Chloe, expecting her to object to the door-to-door interviews, but distress and fatigue had sapped her resistance. She had become detached and unresponsive. Her nerves were frayed.

"Don't worry, Chloe," Clare said optimistically. "We'll get her back."

Brett hoped that his partner was right.

Louise threw up her hands. "Where do I start?"

"How about the code number?" Brett tried to help the jittery recruit.

"All right," she said. "I didn't get anything from the PNC. And no joy with car hire or the manufacturers I've tried so far, I'm afraid. But I had an idea. Hope you don't mind. You know that EOT bit. I wondered if it was the end of Peugeot." Sheepishly, she looked up at Brett and Clare.

Earnestly, Brett nodded. "That's good." He could feel upbeat as long as there was an idea or a theory to test, an obvious way forward. "Did you get on to Peugeot?"

"The technical department was engaged. I'm waiting for Ring Back now. But I haven't chased it any more because there's something else."

75

"Oh?"

"Hilary Garner's home number doesn't start with 775 and neither does Ventura. It's Coventry 779988. But…"

"Go on," Brett urged.

"They've got direct-line numbers to individual workers as well. Not every worker, you know, just managers and the like. All those numbers start with 77."

Brett was impressed with his new assistant. She might have no confidence at all but she scratched away at clues like an old hand. "And what's Hilary Garner's company number?"

"Their switchboard told me it was 773513. Sorry, Brett."

Brett smiled. "We can't blame you for her phone number. Besides, you've got us a real lead. Whoever used that notepad might have been in contact with someone at Ventura by their direct-line number." To Clare, he said, "Hilary Garner goes to the top of our interview list."

"I checked with banks, like you asked. You were right," Louise said in admiration of Brett. "It could be an account number. But only one bank's got that number on its records. It's the account of a man in Norwich."

Brett could tell from Louise's tone that she hadn't finished. "Yes?" he murmured, encouraging her to go on.

"I made a few enquiries by phone. He's a tennis

player. And on Monday he was involved in a tournament at Brighton."

"Into the evening?"

Louise nodded. "He's got a couple of hundred witnesses. The crowd. He lost, though."

"So he won't be topping up his bank account. Good stuff, Louise."

She continued, "There's the dog bites, as well."

Even though the forensic team had not detected any blood at the scene, Brett wanted to pursue every lead. If Copper had got his teeth into Kerry's assailant, the blood could have soaked into clothing or dripped into the car rather than been spilled on to the ground. He asked Louise, "Any more worth chasing?"

"Possibly," she answered. "A health centre up in Chapeltown had a case late last night. A woman. They got no details except her name and address. Pamela Willett. That's the only one."

"OK. We'll go and see what she's like." Brett read her address from Louise's notes. "I'd be interested, to say the least, if she looks like Phil's stalker." He picked up a copy of the artist's sketch and examined it briefly. The woman was white, plain but not unattractive, with dark curly shoulder-length hair. Her round face suggested considerable physical strength. Brett muttered, "I don't recognize her. Can't say I've noticed her around the squash courts." Then he asked Louise, "Is that the lot for now?"

Louise nodded again. She tipped her head to one side to listen conscientiously to Brett's next orders.

"Thanks. You're doing well. We'd be lost without you. Put this sketch out to all South Yorkshire Police stations, and neighbouring ones like your old stomping ground. Let's see if someone else recognizes her. And check it against the police database. I'll organize a team to take it round H-Cars and Phil's other haunts – like his house – in case someone can pin a name on her. What else? Get back to Ventura and try to persuade them to give you a list of all employees with telephone numbers starting with 775. But keep on at Peugeot as well. We can't be sure that code's part of a Ventura phone number, so we've got to keep an open mind, explore other avenues. Besides, we still need an explanation for the EOT. I like the Peugeot idea. Work on it, Louise."

Georeg had worked with DI Lawless previously. The graphologist had analyzed some hand-writing for Brett with perfect accuracy. Because Brett was the sceptical, scientific sort, he did not really believe in George's craft, so it had been a pleasure for George to score a direct hit. He'd enjoyed his brief exchanges with Brett because his success allowed him to taunt the detective. Brett had become an easy target for George's good-natured but barbed gibes.

This time, George summarized his conclusions on the kidnap note for Brett and Clare. "You've got yourselves a left-handed writer. That's for sure. No joy with gender, though. Could be a man or a woman. It's not childish: adult style. There isn't enough here for a thorough interpretation – not that you'd believe me even if there was – but I imagine the writer's goal-minded. Possibly obsessively so. He – or she – *is* whatever he does. A little impulsive and possibly independent. The note was written in a state of excitement."

Given the nature of the message, it was obvious that it would have been written in a state of excitement, Brett thought. He expected George to recognize a left-hander but Brett regarded the remainder of his analysis as mere conjecture, not based on solid physical evidence. Yet he had to acknowledge that George could have been describing a research scientist with an important purpose. Someone like Ross Mundee. Or it could have been a stalker, someone obsessed with Phil. Brett steered the graphologist on to firmer ground. "Whoever wrote the note, did he or she also jot down the EOT and code number?"

"Ah, that's right. You scientists feel more comfortable with comparisons than with informed opinion," George jeered. "But I'm going to disappoint you. It's tricky to decide. Put me in court and I'd have to say there's not enough to match the two. There's nothing in common. No numbers and no capital E, O or T in the kidnap note." He shrugged helplessly. "But, if you want my best bet, for what it's worth, I'd say the same hand *did* do both. Quite possibly."

Greta was more useful. "Before you ask me," she said, "yes, I've got a team on standby for the Princess Street job when we get the all-clear. Now, that syringe. It was used for heroin. And it was covered with the fingerprints of an addict on the drug squad's database. I checked. Apparently, he's known to shoot up in the wood. Unlikely to be anything to do with your Kerry, thank goodness."

Brett was relieved. He wouldn't have known how to tell Phil and Chloe that Kerry had been drugged. "The material?"

"That's a hit. The bite marks correspond with Copper's teeth. But the type of leisure-wear coat it comes from is too common to help. But how about this? There were particles of chalk on it."

"Chalk?" Brett said, surprised. "Good old calcium carbonate?"

"That's the stuff," Greta answered.

"So, we've got a teacher," Clare chipped in with a mischievous grin. She could not take the find seriously. There was little to be deduced, she thought, from the discovery of one of the most common substances on the planet.

"Isn't a lot of blackboard chalk calcium sulphate these days?" Brett asked Greta.

The forensic scientist smiled. "That's what I like. If only all the other cops were on top of the situation like you, Brett. Yes, classroom chalk is usually, but not always, calcium sulphate. So it's unlikely to be a teacher, but you shouldn't rule it out, either."

To convince them that she was only joking, Clare added, "How about a snooker player?"

Brett knew that his partner was kidding but her

comment made him think of another question. "What colour was the chalk?"

"White."

"OK, not a snooker player," Clare said. "Theirs is blue. Perhaps it's someone who's visited the cliffs of Dover recently."

Still keen to extract any possible leads from Greta's findings, Brett said, "Chalk's used as a filler in lots of pills, paper and cosmetics, isn't it? And it's a polishing powder in quite a few toothpastes these days."

"Spot on," Greta agreed. "The biggest industrial use is in making cement but it also goes into putty and crayons." With a sigh, Greta concluded, "I'm with Clare on this one. Chalk's got too many sources. There's too much to aim at." She paused and then continued, "I'll tell you something else that won't help, but it shows how careful we're being. We identified a stick with Copper's bite marks on it as well."

"Now that *is* pretty useless," Brett conceded.

"We're working on the paper and ink of the note now. Nothing yet, except that it's real ink, not biro. I'll let you know when we've done a proper analysis."

"Tyres?" Brett prompted.

"Too many, Brett. I think quite a few dog-walkers must drive their cars on to that patch of ground, treat it like a car park. It's left us with a lot of impressions. But we've got them all on photos and casts. I'll let you know if we can sort out anything worthwhile."

Conveniently, Brett's phone rang to tell him that the arch workshop had been made safe. The damaged wall had been shored up, the workshop ceiling supported with props, the truck stabilized with ropes, and strong nets draped over everything to restrict falling masonry. "That's it," he announced to Greta. "You've got the green light."

Greta nodded. "I'll fetch my gear," she said.

On the way to Chapeltown, Brett and Clare grabbed sandwiches and cans of Coke. Late lunch on the run as usual, at the height of a case. While they were eating in the car, Louise called. At once, her tone betrayed her disappointment. Brett hardly needed to listen to her words to understand the message. Peugeot Cars had denied all knowledge of the code. Brett and Clare drove on. Pamela Willett was not at home. After making a few inquiries with her neighbours, they found her at work. She was a part-time receptionist at a school in Chapeltown. Her left arm was extensively bandaged and she was double Phil's age. Nothing like his stalker. She explained that she had been attacked yesterday when she had challenged a pupil who was acting suspiciously out-side the school after hours. The student's dog had interpreted her intervention as an assault on his owner and become aggressive.

Her story checked out. Both the head teacher and the student gave consistent accounts of the incident, even if the head blamed the boy and his dog while the boy blamed Mrs Willett. Having eliminated Pamela Willett from the inquiry, Brett did not feel obliged to send a photographer to record the bruising on her arm and compare it with the pattern of Copper's teeth.

Getting back into the car, Clare suggested, "Coventry?"

Brett nodded. "It'll only take an hour, just over maybe, if the M1's clear and we don't get caught for speeding."

An hour and fifteen minutes later, they were ushered into an office in Ventura Vehicles, where a male secretary informed them, "Hilary's not at work. He's off sick."

"He?" Clare queried.

The secretary grinned. "Common mistake. Hilary's a man's name as well, you know. Me and him, we both have the same problem. Everyone expects me to be female because I'm a secretary. He's called Hilary so most people think he'll be a woman. Men may be breaking into the secretarial ranks but women don't seem to be making inroads into vehicle engineering." He looked up at Clare and added, "Even if they've got equality in the police force."

Clare exchanged a grimace with Brett.

They wrung Hilary's home address out of his secretary, then went to find his house.

It was a monster on the posh side of the city, on the road to Kenilworth and Warwick. When the manager of Ventura escorted them into his large lounge, the first thing that caught Clare's eye was Miro's abstract painting *Crying Lady with a Cat* on the wall. Lots of gleeful red and brilliant yellow, in the fanciful style of a primary-school child. When Mr Garner noticed Clare's curiosity and admiration, he waved his hand dismissively and said, "Not as impressive as it looks. A copy." He hurried across the room and shut the study door. Just before it closed, Clare glimpsed an even more magnificent work of art in his study: the dark and dazzling *Storm on the Sea of Galilee* by Rembrandt. His only known seascape. Clare was stunned.

"Now," Hilary said, sitting down and waving the detectives towards chairs, "what can I do for you?"

Keeping to the point, Brett asked, "Do you know Phil Chapman?"

"H-Cars," the man from Ventura replied. "In a way, a rival."

"In what way?"

Much more open than Ross Mundee, Garner answered, "Along with our conventional range of vehicles, we have interests in the next generation of cars. Solar-powered cars – mainly for export to sunnier climates – and hydrogen-fuelled vehicles. That's where we overlap with H-Cars. Has something happened to Chapman? I hope not, even if he is slightly ahead of us." His tone was superficially sincere.

Ignoring the question, Brett said, "You admit he's ahead of you. Have you ever tried to poach him?"

"I could use a good man like him, but 'poach' is a provocative word. I once contacted him just to check that he commanded an appropriate salary at H–Cars. I might have mentioned what I could offer here. He seemed happy where he was, so I backed off."

"Have you, or any of your staff, tried to entice him to Ventura since then?"

"No."

Even at home on a hot day, Hilary Garner was wearing a suit and tie. Clare's eyes kept drifting from the smart manager towards the three paintings in the plush room. Along with the Miro masterpiece, there were two other surrealist works that she did not recognize. But one, she believed, bore the distinctive style of a lesser-known Picasso.

Repeating the question that he had used at Sabre, Brett asked, "Your approach to a hydrogen-based car: would it be on-board generation or on-board storage?"

Clare interpreted Hilary Garner's hesitation as surprise at Brett's chemical knowledge rather than reticence or obstruction. "I can say only that we're engaged in storing hydrogen in a metal alloy. But what is all this? Why ask?"

Brett had to come clean. If Garner was the kidnapper, Brett had to make sure he knew that the police had been drawn into an investigation by coincidence. "Someone might be going too far to persuade Phil Chapman to work for them by holding his daughter to ransom," Brett disclosed. "Quite by chance, at the scene of an unrelated accident, a witness saw a little girl being abducted. The description led us to Kerry Chapman."

"I'm sorry to hear that," Hilary murmured. "Now I understand why you wanted to speak to me."

"To be blunt, Mr Garner," Brett said, "we need to know where you were yesterday, about six-thirty in the evening."

Hilary thought about it for a few moments and then replied, "I was here on my own."

Clare gazed at him and asked, "Are you sure?"

Hilary nodded. "Yes."

"Can anyone confirm it?" Brett asked.

"No. I stayed in because I was feeling unwell."

"You haven't been into work yesterday or today. What's the problem?" Clare enquired.

His hand touched the side of his head and he winced theatrically. "Migraine. The sort that knocks me sideways. Impossible to concentrate on anything." He pointed to a bookcase where there was a packet of painkillers.

Brett recognized the tablets as paracetamol mixed with a filler of calcium carbonate. He made a mental note of the medication and changed the direction of the interview. "Does EOT 01203775 mean anything to you?" he queried.

Hilary shook his head slowly. "Nearly a Ventura telephone number." He shrugged. "No. Sorry."

"It's very important," Brett said. He walked up to Garner, repeated the code and handed him a pad.

"Just write it on that for me and take a good look. It might help to see it written down."

Hilary flashed a suspicious glance at Brett but took the proffered notepad and then slipped a fountain pen from his pocket. Awkwardly, he jotted down the number falteringly with his right hand and then examined it. "No," he said. "It doesn't mean anything to me." He returned the pad.

"All right. Thanks. That's more or less enough for now," Brett said. He took down the details of Garner's own car – a distinctive custom-built Ventura – and then left.

Once Clare had driven their car out of view of Garner's house, Brett asked her to stop. "What did you think of him?"

"I didn't believe the migraine attack," she declared. "Or the bit about staying at home on his own. But somehow I can't see him in a casual polyester coat, either."

"Mmm. Maybe not, but what if he was *trying* to look different? Anyway, his car's showy enough to be noticeable. Why don't we ask one or two neighbours about its comings and goings?"

"Because it's too hot and I haven't got any suntan lotion." More seriously, Clare added, "And because we haven't cleared it with Warwickshire Constabulary."

"Oh, let's just get on with it," Brett uttered. "You do one side and I'll do the other. We'll tell the locals if we have to come back and take it further."

Back in the car fifteen minutes later, they compared notes. Between them, they had one sighting of Garner's car leaving the area yesterday after lunch and two statements from neighbours who noticed it returning in the evening between eight-thirty and nine o'clock.

"So much for his migraine," Brett muttered. "It's a cover for something he doesn't want us to know about."

"Are we going back in to confront him?"

"No. Let's look into him a bit more first. Get someone to check the M1 videos for his car in case he drove to Sheffield last night."

"And this morning," Clare commented. "In Attercliffe. We need officers to comb Princess Street, checking if anyone saw his car there."

"True. John'll give us the extra troops. But Garner would have to be pretty stupid to get caught like that. And he isn't. First, though," Brett said, "I want to sort out surveillance, with Warwickshire's co-operation. That's the most important thing. If he's got Kerry, he'll have to go and feed her or whatever. I want a team right behind him whenever he moves."

By the time that Brett had made all the phone calls to organize the next stage of their investigation, they were on the M1 again. He settled back into his seat, glanced at his partner and observed, "You redheads really don't mix with the sun, do you?"

Several times during the day Clare had exposed her sensitive face to the powerful sunshine. It wasn't for long, but it was enough. More than enough. Tentatively, she touched the sunburnt skin on her nose and forehead. It felt tight, as if severely stretched over the bones, and it blazed uncomfortably. In a few days, the damaged skin would peel off like the moulting layers of a snake. "I meant to buy some sun screen in Waters last night but in the heat of the moment I forgot." She glanced in the rear-view mirror and over her shoulder, then she overtook a gargantuan lorry. With a clear lane ahead, she peeked at Brett and, as she drove, told him what was really on her mind. "You know," she remarked, "one of those paintings in Garner's lounge was by Joan Miro. That's the male Joan. Unfortunately, females were painted, not painters, in the 1920s and 1930s. Spanish surrealist. And if I remember rightly, that piece was stolen from Greece a few years back."

"So? He said his was just a copy."

"Yes," Clare murmured hesitantly. "I'm no expert but I wouldn't be so sure. He had some others hidden away, as well. In the study. Didn't want us to see them. But I got a flash of a Rembrandt. One that disappeared from somewhere in America. About 1990. I dread to think what the original's worth. We're talking National Lottery money."

"What is it about you and art? How come you know all this stuff?"

Clare shrugged. "I like paintings. It's an interest. You know I like watching football but you've never asked me to explain that. I'm not sure I could. I just like it."

Brett glanced at his partner and saw reticence in her profile. He decided not to pursue the topic. Instead, he murmured thoughtfully, "It's curious that Garner's got copies of two paintings that have both been stolen. I'll give you that."

"Astonishing, I'd say. The way he shut that door so quickly, I wonder if he's got more premier-division stuff tucked away in his study for his eyes only."

"Possibly," Brett replied. "But I'd be much more interested if he had Kerry tucked away somewhere."

George examined the two pieces of paper side by side. "No," he announced without a hint of doubt. "It's definitely not the same writing as the kidnap note. But this," he said, tapping Brett's notepad with

Hilary Garner's scrawl, "may not be your suspect's normal style. He could've disguised his writing if he knew you were testing him. To be sure, you want a sample of his *normal* writing. You've got to be more subtle than this, Brett," George proclaimed with glee.

"Thanks for the advice," Brett said ironically. "But you're forgetting something. I'll pass it on to Greta. She can compare the two inks."

"You're banking on him keeping to the same pen," George observed, trying to dent Brett's confidence.

"True. He had the pen in a pocket. Probably carries it everywhere, uses it for everything." Brett had much more faith in a chemical analysis than in graphology.

On the way to see Phil and Chloe, Brett called Louise to get the latest news from her. Inside the Chapmans' house, the atmosphere was taut and ominous, like the breathless calm before a storm. Phil and Chloe might have been rowing or maybe they were obstinately refusing to speak to each other, having retreated into their own worlds. Perhaps they had merely run out of words to describe their predicament. In this charged and overcast setting, Brett had to confess that he'd made little progress. He had far more questions than answers. Door-to-door enquiries in the neighbourhood had not shed any light on who had delivered the note. The sketch of Phil's female stalker didn't match anyone in the police database. A couple of

Phil's colleagues at H-Cars had seen her hanging around the factory but they had no idea who she was. Tracing the victims of dog bites had led to a dead end. But the Ventura angle was hopeful and Garner did not have an alibi. Even more intriguing was the fact that he had lied about his movements. He was hiding something.

"Hilary Garner," Phil said thoughtfully, as if he were tasting the name like wine in his mouth.

"What do you think?" asked Brett.

Phil shrugged. "No idea. Don't know him well enough. All I know is, he's loaded and his hydrogen car's going nowhere. He could well be desperate for progress. He knows I'll beat him to the chequered flag."

Chloe exploded. "How dare you brag about work when Kerry's – It's your rotten work that got us into this!"

Stepping into the fray, Brett said, "No, Chloe. I *want* Phil to talk about it. It's important. Maybe it sounds heartless but I need to know. Phil's research might lead us to whoever's behind this."

Chloe looked the other way and declined to say any more. She had become withdrawn, reduced only to emotional outbursts. It seemed that the pain threatened to tear Chloe and Phil apart.

Awkwardly, Brett carried on. "Garner talked about storing hydrogen in a metal alloy," he said to Phil. "Is that the trick?"

Phil had lost the ability to smile. His face was

sunken and stressed. Yet he managed a wry expression where, a couple of days ago, he would have bellowed with laughter. "Alloys! That's what I *told* him the trick was. But I'll let you into a secret. It's got nothing to do with metals. I put him on to that method to waste his time. It won't work." He cast a sidelong, nervous glance at Chloe before continuing, "*My* car'll travel over a thousand miles on a single tank of hydrogen, stored in tiny graphite fibres. And I can make them super-cheap. That's the future: a clean fuel held in microscopic carbon tubes, but no one knows yet. And you won't tell the opposition."

"You know I won't," Brett replied.

Brett downed the rest of his pint and sighed. "We haven't made much progress," he said restlessly.

"We've got plenty of leads," Clare countered, trying to shift his bleak mood.

"I know. That's normally enough for me after a day or two. But not this time. Because of the threat to Kerry. Is she OK? Is she hurt? Never mind catching whoever's taken her: right now I'd settle for finding her safe and sound. I'm not sure how much longer Phil and Chloe can take it. We're no closer to her than when we started. Our best break's been the derailed train. Hardly good detective work. Just coincidence."

"Don't knock good luck," Clare retorted. "On the beat, where I was for a lot longer than you, you'd be surprised how often we'd nab someone by sheer good luck. We'd go to a domestic and find stolen tellies, arrest someone for drink driving and find they were wanted for mugging. Good luck's all part of the game. You take it whenever you can get it."

"We shouldn't need it. We've got suspects and some solid evidence if only we could put it all together. The polyester coat, hydrogen, chalk, left-handedness, the code, the handwriting."

"Perhaps when we get stuff from Princess Street and the tyre impressions..."

Brett glanced at his watch. It was nearly ten o'clock. Outside it was almost dark. "Before I call it a day, I'm going to drive up to Barnsley and see if Alan Fox is at home," he announced.

Clare finished her ale. "You're putting a lot of emphasis on the hydrogen–car angle. What about this stalker?"

"I don't know. I can get inside scientists' brains, see their motivation and their motives maybe, but I can't figure out a stalker. Can you? You sounded pretty knowledgeable in the wood last night. Have you ever worked on a stalking case?"

"Once or twice," Clare informed him. "Tricky to handle."

"Well? Are we dealing with one here or is it just professional jealousies? I guess I'm worried in case Phil's stalker *is* behind it. She'll know Phil's habits inside out. Might even have seen me playing squash with him. Though there's no reason to think she'd know I'm in the police. But if she's such an expert at surveillance, she might be keeping watch on us somehow."

Clare shook her head. "Don't get paranoid. Your inexperience is showing again. Stalkers are hopeless at surveillance. Otherwise, their victims wouldn't know they were victims. Stalkers just loiter and linger awkwardly, sticking out like sore thumbs. They're persistent, obsessive and blinkered – the ones I came across were, anyway – and spend all their spare time and energy pursuing their quarry. They devote themselves to a single unrealistic goal. They're sad individuals. Not great communicators. The psychologists say they'll do more or less *anything* to get the attention of their victim – who they say they love. In one of my cases, the stalker sent bits of himself in the post: hair, shavings, nail clippings. At least Phil's admirer has stopped short of sending a severed finger."

"Charming," Brett murmured.

"Actually, Phil's stalker's in a minority. Most of them chase ex-partners because they can't cope with the separation. A quarter are well known to their targets but were never romantically involved with them. Neither fits Phil's situation. Only ten per cent of stalkers are complete strangers to their victims. My second case was like that as well: a male stalker who followed his female target *everywhere*. He saw her boyfriend as a rival. Set fire to his car, smashed all the windows in his flat, that sort of thing. The target herself was afraid to go out, lost her boyfriend.

Lost any sort of normal life. You see, being stalked is a slow form of torture. And sometimes stalkers attack: attempted murder. I guess the logic is, 'If I can't have her – or him – no one else will.' After that, there's suicide. The ultimate act of devotion to a dead loved one."

"Worrying," Brett murmured. "But until Phil's stalker surfaces again, I can't do any more to identify her. Maybe we don't need to while there's plenty of mileage in the hydrogen-car theory."

Clare's eyebrows arched upwards. "You're putting industrial rivalry before stalking, then? Is that wise? Remember, Phil's stalker hasn't put in an appearance for a few days. Why not? She might be coping with a kidnap."

"I'm well aware of that," Brett answered. "I'm not ignoring the stalker but I've got to be practical. Look, we've got two theories. Industrial secrets and stalking. I'm just admitting that one's easier to test than the other at the moment. There's no point dwelling on a theory you can't test."

"All right, Brett. But let's not get carried away with your chemistry and forget the stalker. I've got a sneaking suspicion—"

"And no evidence," Brett remarked, standing up and digging in his trouser pocket for his car key.

Clare sighed and shook her head. Until a cop's intuition could be measured and presented in court, she knew that she wouldn't be able to persuade Brett to take it seriously. Without disguising the bitterness in her voice, she said, "If you handle Alan Fox on your own, I'll try and contact someone about stolen paintings. At this time of night, it won't be easy. I'll have to try and get hold of home numbers."

"You're relying on another lucky break. You've questioned someone about an abduction and you want to solve the mystery of the missing masterpieces. Let's not get carried away with art and forget Kerry."

"I'm not," she retorted. "I bet you'd like a good reason for bugging Garner, though, and maybe I can provide it."

"All right. Thanks. It's a deal," Brett replied in a conciliatory tone. With a dry smile, he added, "I'll visit Fox, you talk to Rembrandt."

Clare stood up. Before she left, she said, "If you want, you can join me for a nightcap at my place. I'll tell you what he said. And you can tell me what Fox said."

Brett nodded appreciatively. "Thanks. I'd like that. See you later."

Alan Fox lived in the Kingstone district of Barnsley but he was not at home. Tirelessly pursuing the case, Brett quizzed Fox's next-door neighbour who suggested a trawl of the local pubs. She was right. Eventually, Brett found Alan Fox playing darts for his pub team. It was nearly closing time when he asked the landlord to point out the vehicle engineer. Brett bought himself a drink. For several minutes, he watched his suspect from the bar. His first impressions were discouraging. Alan Fox threw with his right hand and, when he chalked up his score on the blackboard, he crossed his sevens. In the code number, the sevens had not been crossed.

At the end of the game, which Alan won, he came to the bar to order a last beer. The landlord said to him, "Well played. It's all up to Ed Tarrant, then."

Alan nodded. "Yeah. It's all on the last game now. And Ed's not in the best of moods after his burglary last week. Keep your fingers crossed he can forget it and concentrate on his darts." He rested his back and both elbows on the bar as he prepared to watch the final leg of the match. He was dressed in a loose shirt and tracksuit bottoms.

When Brett stepped up and introduced himself, flashing his ID, Alan looked puzzled and then amused. He raised his glass and muttered, "You'll be pleased to know I'm not driving home. I'm a cyclist."

"A vehicle engineer who cycles, eh?"

"A vehicle engineer who keeps fit and doesn't pollute the place without good cause," Alan replied, keeping his eye on the darts match. "Why?"

"I heard you were interested in green cars."

"So what?" Then he yelled out, "Go on, Ed!"

"Do you know Phil Chapman?"

"Biggest bragger in the business, Chapman. But I suppose he's every right to be. He could be the best."

"I imagine you'd like to have him at Morlands."

Briefly, Alan looked away from the match and stared at Brett. "Sure. I talked to him about it but didn't get anywhere. What's he done?"

"Nothing," Brett replied.

"What's someone done to *him*, then?"

"Do you know Princess Street in Sheffield?" asked Brett, purposely avoiding Alan's question.

"Princess Street? I don't think so."

Clare was a better judge of character than Brett and he wished that she was with him to see Fox's reactions. To Brett, he seemed to be genuine. "I ask because I'm investigating a witness's sighting of an abduction in that area, related to Phil Chapman."

Alan was not paying much attention. Abruptly, he cried, "Good darts!"

"Where were you yesterday evening, six till seven?"

Alan turned to Brett and declared angrily, "If that's an accusation, tough. I don't know anything about it. I was out cycling, so I've got an alibi."

"You've got an alibi if someone saw you. Did anyone?"

"More than that. Someone tried to splatter me in the road like a hedgehog. Turned left in front of me. I hit his side and came off. Luckily I was OK, and the bike only got a puncture. Just as well because it was brand new. The car didn't stop, of course. It was a red Toyota Carina. I took his number. N707 NBD. Trace him and I've got my alibi, and you can book him for dangerous driving while you're at it."

"And how will I know it was—"

Interrupting, Alan groaned aloud. "Damn! That's us sunk." He exchanged a pained expression with the landlord. "Seven-six," he complained as the opposition players celebrated their last-gasp victory. Downcast, Alan grimaced at Brett and said impatiently, "You'll know it was me all right because he'll have some rubber from my bike tyre on the paintwork of his front passenger door."

Clare could hardly contain her outrage. "I never knew the problem was so bad," she said. "I'm amazed. So much of our heritage has just vanished." She had managed to contact the operations manager of the Art Loss Register and she began to recite what she had learned. "There are more than two thousand works of art missing. Nicked. That's a massive hole in our art collections. And we're not just talking unknowns. Three hundred and twelve Picassos, a hundred and twenty Rembrandts, another hundred and twenty Dalis, and so it goes on. Toulouse-Lautrec, Andy Warhol, Turner, over two hundred Miros."

Brett was also taken aback by the extent of the swindle, but he was distracted by his concern for Kerry.

"There's someone I ought to speak to, apparently," Clare continued. "DI Jack Fitzgerald of the central London crime squad, a specialist in missing works of art. I'll call him tomorrow when we've got a minute."

Hinting, Brett began, "I thought you were —"

Clare sprang to her feet. "Sorry. I forgot. I promised you a nightcap. I was upset."

With a wry smile, Brett commented, "I could tell."

Halfway to the kitchen, Clare stopped and exclaimed, "*Storm on the Sea of Galilee* – the Rembrandt that Garner had – is priceless."

Miserably, Brett added, "So is Kerry."

Over a drink, Clare loosened up. "Earlier, you asked me why the interest in painting. I guess there *is* a reason. I suppose you deserve to hear it. There was this chap. A painter I went out with once. I suppose he got me interested."

"Was it serious?" Brett asked.

"Depends what you mean," she replied evasively. "But he was OK." With her eyes, she said much more than OK.

"What happened?"

"It didn't work out, his brush with the law." Her smile was tinged with regret, even pain. "I couldn't give him as much time as he wanted. And he got his artistic inspiration by using substances I should've arrested him for possessing."

"Ah. The old problem – conflict of interests. A choice between boyfriend and career, but not both. And you went for career."

Clare nodded sadly. "All I got out of it was a still life." She looked across the lounge where a painting of a vase of flowers occupied a prominent place on the wall.

Obviously, the artist had once occupied a prominent place in Clare's life. Brett felt concerned for her but he did not pry any more. It would have felt too much like an investigation of his partner's private life.

Brett was tormented by images of Kerry. A small girl crying alone in the dark, frightened, thirsty, hungry. Perhaps she had a gag in her mouth. Perhaps she was tied up. Perhaps she had been sedated. Perhaps...

She had been away from home for thirty hours. Other than that note, there had been no word from her captors. The silence aggravated and disturbed him. If her kidnapper intended to extract something from Phil, surely the demand would arrive soon. It would come as a relief – and provide another clue. In the middle of the night it struck Brett that he'd been blinkered in his reasoning. If the motive for the crime concerned Phil and his job, what about the personnel of H-Cars? Perhaps there were internal jealousies. But what if it had nothing at all to do with Phil?

Perhaps it was more to do with Chloe. Perhaps someone had a reason for wanting to hurt her. Or perhaps Kerry had unwittingly made herself an enemy. Perhaps...

When Brett finally fell asleep, his mind was full of uncomfortable possibilities. He feared for his godchild.

Professor Derek Jacob had been one of Brett's tutors when he took his degree in biochemistry at the University of Sheffield. When Brett and Clare walked unannounced into his office on Wednesday morning, he had his feet propped up on his desk. With both of his hands round a mug of black coffee, he was reading the magazine on his lap. Surprised, the chemist exclaimed, "Brett Lawless! And partner Clare. How are things in the real world? Have you brought me some gruesome body fluids to analyze again?" In two of Brett's previous cases Derek's expertise had provided vital clues. He had become an occasional but invaluable resource for Brett's investigations.

Nodding towards the mug and the journal, Brett said, "Things are just as hectic as ever in the academic world then?"

Derek laughed. "It comes to something, you know, when I feel guilty about taking ten minutes out to read *Analytical Chemistry*. But I do. Keeping up with literature is an essential part of the job. Sitting, thinking and reading is what we used to do. Now it's a luxury, crammed into break time, evenings and weekends. How's lawlessness?"

"Getting worse," Brett replied, taking a seat. "Remember Phil Chapman?"

"Yes. Bright, but at the back of the queue when they dished out modesty. Not much left when his turn came." He put his feet down, selected two mugs and peered inside them. "There's more hazardous substances in here than in the lab. Want a coffee? The boiling water will kill off whatever's growing inside."

"No, thanks," Brett answered. "We've only got a couple of minutes. I'm just after a bit of information." He explained Phil's situation to Derek and then asked, "Is there anyone here in the university working with local industry on environmentally friendly fuels? Especially if it's Sabre."

"Not in chemistry," Derek replied soberly. "But there's a chap in the technology department: Naoki Matsumoto. Japanese, if you hadn't guessed. You might want to speak to him."

"Do you know if he's got any industrial contacts? An engineer called Ross Mundee, for instance?"

"No idea," Derek said, draining his mug. "He's supposed to be very brainy, and equally bonkers. I don't like him. Gives academics a bad name, acting the nutty fanatical professor. Only it's not an act. He's got a couple of huge grants recently. One for developing hydrogen as a fuel, the other in robotics. Obviously versatile as well."

Brett thanked his old tutor and headed directly for the technology faculty. Without undergraduate students, the place was peculiarly quiet. In one of the endless, dingy corridors, Brett and Clare stopped. They had both caught sight of a cockroach. It scurried across the floor past Clare and then came to a complete, inexplicable halt. By instinct, she lifted her trainer to stamp on it, but hesitated. At the same time, Brett grabbed her arm and cried, "No!" Its odd behaviour and appearance had convinced Brett that it was no ordinary cockroach.

Frowning, Brett knelt down and examined the weird insect. He was right. Instead of wings, it had a small electronic component strapped to its back like a haversack.

Almost at once, a small bespectacled man emerged from one of the laboratories and dashed towards them, screeching, "Leave Robbie alone!" He squatted down beside Brett and cried, "You nearly put paid to half a million pounds' worth of research!"

"What is it?" Brett enquired.

Professor Matsumoto put it on the palm of his hand and said with a quirky grin, "Robotroach. Robbie, for short. Half robot, half cockroach. An insect controlled remotely by electrical impulses. Forward or back, left or right, fast or slow."

"What's that on its back? The controller?"

Naoki smiled proudly. "Not just that. It's a miniature video camera and microphone." He stood up, keeping his eye on his precious hybrid. "Who are you, anyway?" In his enthusiasm, he had forgotten to question the strangers in his department.

Brett introduced himself and Clare. "How come it escaped into the corridor?" Brett asked, fascinated by the insect.

"He didn't. I was testing him. Halfway to a proper field trial. Watching people coming and going. You were the only ones to spot him. Perhaps it's true that police officers are observant."

On the way back to the engineer's office, Clare asked, "Why have you done that to the poor thing?" She was repulsed by the manipulation of a living being, albeit a cockroach. Not a species that she was fond of, but still a creature that deserved a life free from slavery.

"In Japan," Professor Matsumoto explained fervently, "we have lots of earthquakes. Just think about a small team of these cockroaches on the scene. They'll go anywhere. Over any terrain, into the smallest holes, and transmit pictures back – once I improve the camera technology so it gives better images in the dark. Excellent for finding people trapped in the most inaccessible and dangerous places where a normal robot can't go because it's too big." The impassioned justification of his work suggested that he was obsessed with it.

Both Clare and Brett thought of the devastated and perilous Princess Street site but said nothing. Neither of them was prepared to argue against Naoki's invention when it had the potential to save lots of lives like Kerry's.

In the computer-filled office, Naoki asked, "What can I do for you?"

"It's your other research work I'm interested in. Hydrogen-based vehicles." Without giving all of the details, Brett explained the reason for his visit and the Chapmans' predicament.

"I know Dr Chapman. I spoke to him at a conference once. A smart man." With the frankness of an academic, Naoki continued, "I believe he bragged a little. He was a bit too eager to discuss his ideas about metal alloys. If I'm not mistaken, he was trying to lay a false trail. As you English say, lead me up your garden path." He tried to summon a smile at Phil's subterfuge, but it wasn't very convincing.

"Did you resent his attitude?"

"I can't say I appreciated his gamesmanship, but there's a lot at stake. I understand his competitiveness."

Brett continued, "I really came to ask if you know a Ross Mundee at Sabre."

"Certainly," Naoki answered. "A fine, generous industrialist."

"So," Brett said, "you get funds from him. What do you think of him?"

Naoki considered the question for a moment. Again, he seemed to answer frankly. "Not especially social, no great sense of humour. Serious and determined. He's not so subtle in his research thinking. When he comes across an obstacle, he tends to try and blast his way through it rather than find the smart way round it."

"Single-minded in pursuit of a goal," Brett summarized.

"Exactly."

"Did you see him, or contact him, yesterday or the day before?"

"Monday or Tuesday? No, I didn't see him. But I tried to call him first thing yesterday. I got his answering machine."

Brett nodded. It reminded him that he had got the same response when a witness had seen an adult in the Princess Street workshop. "Have you ever received handwritten notes from him?"

"I should think so."

Brett requested an example and then tried to remain unruffled as Naoki turned his office upside down to find one. Eventually, the scatty professor admitted defeat. "Doesn't look like I kept anything on paper. It would've been ages ago anyway. We use e-mail now."

Brett sighed. "OK. Never mind. How about this? Some sort of code number. EOT 01203775. Does it mean anything to you in hydrogen-fuel research?"

Naoki shook his head. "The only thing I can think of is a purchase-order number. A part number, maybe."

Brett grimaced. The idea was too vague to follow up. There were too many products and too many suppliers to explore. Instead, he asked, "What about Alan Fox? Morlands in Barnsley. Ever heard of him?"

"Not someone I've come across," Naoki answered. "And I wouldn't approach Morlands anyway. They're competitors of Sabre and I wouldn't want to upset my sponsor, would I?"

"It strikes me," Clare said as they strode towards headquarters, "that Professor Matsumoto is wedded to his work, too. I bet he'd like Phil's secrets. And he's definitely sore about that chat with Phil. What about Matsumoto as a suspect? Did you notice he was left-handed?"

"Yes, I noticed," Brett replied. "Like ten per cent of the population. But, yes, he could go on the list."

Inside, the incident room was quiet. Before Brett had set out for the university, he'd assigned tasks to his team. His officers were out on the streets with likenesses of Phil's stalker and of Kerry. Some were probing sightings that would probably turn out to be false alarms. Others were touring Princess Street with descriptions of Ross Mundee and Hilary Garner, and Garner's car. Officers with informants were out listening to what was happening in the criminal world, hoping for a whisper about a kidnap. Two of his team were working on Louise's list of five Ventura employees with telephone numbers beginning with 775. None of the names had grabbed Brett's attention but he'd instructed his officers to check if any had criminal records or links with the Chapmans. In a different room, two more staff were laboriously sifting videos from the M1 for any sign of

Garner's car – a boring and thankless task, but essential. Brett stood in front of a flip chart with a felt-tip pen in his hand. Thoughtfully, he began to develop his list of suspects along with their likely motives, any evidence against them and their unconfirmed alibis. He put Hilary Garner and Ross Mundee at the top. Then came the unknown stalker. Her entry was depressingly devoid of information. At the bottom, he wrote *Alan Fox, Naoki Matsumoto, Enemies of Chloe*, and *Enemies of Kerry*. On the same chart he jotted down his meagre pieces of evidence so they could be matched against the suspects.

While Clare phoned the central London crime squad and Louise hunted the owner of the red Toyota through its registration number, Brett took a pencil and drew in all of the links between the suspects and the evidence. When he had finished, one suspect had more connections than any of the others. The spider at the tangled heart of his web turned out to be Hilary Garner.

Clare reported on her phone call while Brett stood by the flip chart like a teacher listening to a student. "This Jack Fitzgerald is really interesting," she said. "A guru of art theft."

"Thinking of applying for a transfer and deserting me?" As soon as Brett had made the light-hearted comment, he regretted it. After his partner had been denied a promotion that she believed she deserved, she had felt rejected. She might well be contemplating her future within the force. A change of direction might seem quite attractive to her. With her interest in art, and her fond memories of a painter, she could well be drawn to the investigation of its theft. Brett didn't want to lose her.

For an instant, a frown flashed across Clare's face and then she grinned. "I couldn't do that. You'd never cope without me."

Brett returned her smile but her playful denial did not convince him.

Louise looked up from her computer screen shyly. She detected the small crack that had just opened up between her superiors and was troubled like a child who has just realized that all is not entirely well between her parents.

"Anyway," Clare continued, "Jack's pretty nifty. Recently, he raided a lockup garage in Hampstead and found two hundred pieces, including eighteen Old Masters by Rubens, Gainsborough and Vermeer. Incredible haul. He arrested the gang of eight thieves. Apparently, these types of gangs are really cultured. They go for valuable targets, no rubbish, and do lots of research and reconnaissance before taking on a job. Sometimes they steal to order for wealthy clients. More often they exchange paintings for drugs. They vary their tactics, he said, but quite often they get jobs as caretakers in galleries, or befriend people with private art collections. They usually have at least one member who's an expert in alarm systems so, once they're trusted insiders, it's easy for them to cut the alarms and videos. Then they walk out with the goods. Just like that. At one gallery, he told me, the gang he's just arrested pretended to be builders and erected scaffolding and a screen around the front door so no one could see them going in and bringing out the paintings, complete with frames. Very professional. Very bold."

"And how does all this help Kerry?" Brett enquired stiffly. "Does it gives us anything more on Garner?"

Clare did not want to admit that she wasn't much further forward. "Jack wasn't aware of a Midlands connection. He's looking into it. He's going to tempt Garner with a stolen Dürer, valued at £7,000. See if he bites. It won't be enough to justify a phone tap but he can get him bugged."

"Good. Pity invoices don't change hands on these deals. I'd love to see him write, 'Received with thanks'. Then we'd have a better comparison of his handwriting, and spelling." Brett sighed and then returned to his list. "You know," he said, airing his thoughts aloud, "there's something missing here. If one of these people took Kerry, how did they know about the disused bike workshop in Attercliffe? They wouldn't have taken her there if they hadn't planned it. Louise," he said, "chase the people who used to work there, will you? It'll be difficult because I bet they were moonlighting. Probably claiming unemployment benefit as well. But you can make a good start internally. Apparently, a few weeks ago, we charged the owners with handling stolen goods. Find out who they are and if they've named anyone who worked for them. Even better if they can name customers as well. A list of names could be very interesting."

On a second chart, Brett wrote, *How did the kidnapper know about the workshop?* He paused and then scrawled, *Why did he move Kerry out?* To Clare and Louise, he said, "Without being clairvoyant, he didn't know a train was about to derail. So why did he leave?"

"Because it was just a temporary holding place," Clare ventured.

"Agreed," Brett said. "So was our kidnapper organizing a new hideaway on Monday night? It makes sense. Dump Kerry in a horrible workshop for a night and scare her silly to tame her. Collect her next morning and take her somewhere else. She'd be grateful and compliant, maybe."

Clare shrugged. "It's possible."

"I hope so," Brett murmured, "because, if he did, Greta might find some traces transferred from the new place to the workshop."

"Among all that junk, that's asking a lot," Clare said dismally.

"I know," Brett replied. "But for Kerry's sake, I'm trying to think positively."

The Chapmans were inconsolable. Trying to conduct a normal inquiry in the charged atmosphere, Brett said to Phil, "Thinking about your work, we've been concentrating on your competitors, but we could be wrong. Is there anyone at H-Cars who's jealous of your success, or your family?"

"I don't think so," he answered. "If you want, you can ask Ron – my boss, Ron Peake – in case he's spotted something going on behind my back."

"OK, I'll do that." To Chloe, Brett said gingerly, "I know you think it's all to do with Phil and his research but we shouldn't ignore the possibility that it's something else. Is there anyone who might want to hurt you, via Kerry, for *any* reason?"

"Me?" Chloe exclaimed. "I can't think of anything like that, no."

"What about someone with a grudge against Kerry?"

"She's seven, Brett! Too young for grudges. And you know she's not like that." Chloe could not go on.

"I do know, yes," Brett replied softly. "She's not one to get into trouble. I'm just covering all possibilities."

Copper sat up and barked. Immediately after, there came the clatter of the letter box. Phil dragged himself out of his chair and went to collect the mail.

Brett said to Chloe, "Get in touch with me straightaway if you think of anything."

From the hallway, Phil's startled voice exclaimed, "It's Kerry's writing!"

Brett, Clare and Chloe all jumped up at the same time. Brett was the first to shout, "Don't touch it!"

"I'll go for the postman," Clare said. She ran towards the back door.

Brett knelt down by the mat and examined the letter without touching it. The address was the untidy but legible writing of a child. The cancellation on the first-class stamp was badly smudged. Brett looked at Phil and said, "Posted yesterday but I can't read where. Anyway, you're bothered more about what's inside. Have you got some clean kitchen gloves and a paper knife?"

Back in the living room, Brett sat at the table and prepared to slit open the envelope. Phil and Chloe stood anxiously on either side of him. Clare joined them, saying, "I caught him. Got his name and address."

Brett sliced through the top of the envelope and gingerly removed the folded letter. To Brett it looked like the same paper as the previous note. Clumsy in the ill-fitting gloves, he opened up the letter. They all peered at the brief message scrawled in the same immature writing as the address on the envelope. Three of the words had been attempted, crossed out and rewritten before Kerry had completed them successfully.

I am all right. Everything will be fine if Dad comes to his senses and is ready to give something up. I will write again. Love, Kerry.

Bewildered, Chloe and Phil gazed at each other, then they both stared at Brett.

Brett sighed. "No clear demands yet. But at least she's OK." He squeezed Chloe's arm. "That's the main thing. She says she's all right."

"That's what she's been told to say," Chloe cried. "Like the rest of it. She was forced to write it. Maybe she's…"

Trying to calm his wife, Phil went to her and put his arms around her, a long overdue gesture. Firmly, he said, "She wouldn't write it if she wasn't all right. I'm sure. Even if she was told to."

Chloe's shoulders shook with the force of her sobbing.

After she had dabbed at her eyes with a handkerchief, Brett said, "It looks like this *is* all about you,

Phil. Come to your senses and give something up. Any ideas?"

Phil left a supportive arm around Chloe's shoulders as he replied, "I don't know. But it sounds like someone who's already tried to get me to tell them about my research. Someone who wants me to reveal my methods."

Brett nodded. "Garner, Fox or Mundee," he stated. "Perhaps we *are* barking up the right tree with your competitors, but the message isn't specific enough to be sure. I still need to look at the other possibilities, like Ron Peake. Have you got another polythene bag?" he enquired. "I want to take the letter straight to forensics. And Chloe, can you take Clare to get a couple of things that only Kerry touches? Her toothbrush and something like a comb, say. We'll try and get fingerprints off them to compare with any on this paper and envelope. If we find prints that aren't Kerry's, we might be in luck." Brett was not optimistic, though. He guessed that Kerry's captor had told her to write the letter and to address the envelope to avoid providing any more clues. He even suspected that Kerry had been told to stick the stamp on to the envelope because its positioning was crooked. That way, her kidnapper deprived Brett of a dried saliva sample that would have contained blood-group substances.

Upstairs, Brett put an end to the surveillance operation. "I think I'm wasting your time, Adam. Looks like the messages are going to come in by normal mail. Our kidnapper's being very cautious, getting Kerry to do the writing. He or she isn't the type to phone and allow us to trace the call or give us a voice sample. I suppose you might as well leave the phone bug in place just in case, but you can pack up and go. Thanks for your help anyway."

"My pleasure. It's been a thrill a minute," Adam replied sarcastically.

In forensics, Brett handed over the letter, saying, "Throw everything you've got at it, Greta. Ink, paper, saliva on the envelope, traces, anything. Only Kerry and the postman touched it for sure, so anything else will be useful, to say the least."

"You'll get Kerry's saliva and prints off these," Clare said, giving Greta a bag containing a toothbrush, comb and a book belonging to Kerry. "And this is the postman's name and address. I told him we'd send someone for his dabs."

"Sometimes, you know, it's difficult to get kids' fingerprints. The chemicals that come off their fingers evaporate from surfaces much quicker than the heavy stuff that adults deposit. So we may not have a problem with her dabs obscuring anyone else's. Anyway, I'll get on to it straightaway," Greta promised. "But right now, you want a summary of all the other stuff so far, I suppose."

"Please."

"OK," she said. "The first kidnap note. The paper's classic Basildon and the ink's Parker. Garner used a Parker as well but it's too common to be particularly significant. Then there's the tyre impressions in the wood: sorry, Brett, but there were just too many and not enough quality imprints. The ground was too hard. The best-preserved ones were old, caked by the sun. Getting something from the treads was like doing an incomplete jigsaw when the pieces are mixed in with at least ten other jigsaw puzzles."

Putting aside his disappointment, Brett asked, "Any Princess Street data?"

"Well, the first thing to report is that we discovered something you already know."

"What's that?"

"It was filthy. We've got fingerprints, fragments of glass, dried mud off someone's shoe, and partial shoe impressions in the dust – probably yours, and smaller ones that may be Kerry's. And smaller ones still – a dog's paw marks."

Brett chipped in, "That was me as well. We took Kerry's dog."

"OK," Greta said, downgrading the analysis of the paw impressions. "We got a rusty toolbox and quite a few different human hairs. I'll check against the hairs on Kerry's comb to find which are hers. Then there was a goat hair."

"Goat?" Brett queried.

"That's right. Doesn't mean a goat's been kept there, or we'd have got lots more of its hairs. Someone who's been in contact with a goat has been in the place, that's all. And there are quite a few goats in

Sheffield. Up at Graves Park, there's a sanctuary full of them, for example. What else?" Greta mumbled to herself. "A rope with some human skin on it, used to tie her up? A couple of cigarette ends, a pound coin, and paper from newspapers to sweet wrappers. A small piece of dry straw. Plenty of bits of bikes. Some paint, the sort used on bikes, and flakes of polystyrene, possibly from a cycle helmet. A battered old dart board and a dart flight. Before you ask, yes, we'll check the flight for prints. Two cheap biros, a lens cloth—"

Cutting in, Brett asked, "You mean one of those cloths for cleaning glasses?"

"That's it. But, before you arrest every left-handed person with glasses, remember it could have come from anywhere. It could have blown in off the street."

"Anything else?"

"Plenty. How long have you got? But I think I've covered the main finds. There was a lot more but I'm not convinced it's relevant – it was buried under such a lot of muck. Like a small rusting key to a filing cabinet and a grubby paracetamol pill. They've been there too long to give us anything on Kerry. I'm getting the team to put the effort in on the items that appear to be recent additions. Agreed?"

Brett nodded. "Sure."

By lunchtime, Brett's team had drawn a blank. There had been no sightings of Garner's car or Mundee in

Princess Street and no one else claimed to have noticed Kerry being taken to or away from the workshop. No whispers on the street. Garner's car did not feature in the videos of northbound traffic on the M1 recorded on Monday evening and Tuesday morning by a camera between junctions twenty-eight and twenty-nine. If Hilary Garner had driven to Sheffield, he'd used minor roads. Louise had traced the owner of the red car with the registration N707 NBD. He had confessed to cutting up a cyclist on Monday evening, just after six o'clock. Interestingly, though, he could not describe the cyclist well, and the collision had occurred on the A61, about halfway between Barnsley and Sheffield. If it was Alan Fox on the bicycle, he was only about six miles away from the site of the kidnap. Not far at all for a good cyclist.

Ron Peake sympathized with Phil's situation but he still adopted a hard-line attitude. If Kerry's kidnapper offered to trade Phil's invention for Kerry, he insisted that Phil should protect H-Cars' interests. "Phil doesn't have to remain silent, of course. I suggest he thinks up plausible but fake details to trade. Like his metal-alloy work that didn't get anywhere. The real project is too important to give away."

"And if the kidnapper doesn't buy the bluff?" Brett queried. "Or checks it out before agreeing to release Kerry?"

Ron shrugged. "Phil's good at bluffing. And he's got the time to come up with a particularly effective red herring."

"So, as far as you're concerned, your hydrogen-based car is more important than Kerry Chapman?" Brett asked, not bothering to disguise the exasperation in his tone.

"How many lives do you think a pollution-free car will save? It's a *very* important development and I can't allow it to be hijacked."

"If this was just about saving the environment, you'd give your results to every manufacturer, Mr Peake," Brett objected. "That would be the humanitarian option. That would benefit the environment most, by letting everyone use the technology. But this isn't just about being green, is it? It's about keeping a monopoly on the invention for as long as possible to maximize profits. You're putting profit before Kerry Chapman." Brett decided that, if it came to it, he would be prepared to exchange what he knew about Phil's research in return for his goddaughter. He felt like threatening Ron Peake with leaking the secret of the graphite tubes right now so there was no need for Kerry's abductor to continue holding her, but he would have got Phil into a lot of trouble with his boss. Besides, Brett had promised to keep the information to himself. He would keep his promise unless he felt that Kerry's life was clearly in danger. Then, sacrificing a promise and H-Cars' profits seemed to Brett to be a small price. Of course, Brett hoped that Phil would put his daughter's needs before Ron Peake's demands long before the extortion got out of hand.

Ron said, "I don't for one minute believe that any-one would kill a small girl for our industrial secrets. So, I'm not putting H-Cars' interests before her. Perhaps there'll be a short delay in getting her back because Phil won't reveal our real method, but that's all, I imagine."

Brett was not so convinced. He believed that Kerry was already in jeopardy. All too easily the circumstances could escalate. But he was not going to shift the manager's opinion so he changed tack and asked if there was anyone within H-Cars who might envy Phil enough to abduct his daughter.

Ron breathed in deeply and then exhaled slowly as he pondered the question. "No," he decided. "One or two might be envious of his success, but not *that* envious – or resentful. One or two might be irritated by his pride and – let's be honest – arrogance, but again not *that* irritated."

"All right," Brett said. "Thanks for your help." He left his telephone number with the manager. "If anything strikes you later, tell me straightaway."

In the incident room, a call came in from Jack Fitzgerald but he wanted to speak to Brett, not to Clare. Jack announced that Hilary Garner had shown an interest in the stolen painting that he'd dangled in front of the Ventura manager. Things were moving quickly. Garner had agreed to a meeting in north London at five o'clock to discuss the bogus deal. Brett said, "OK, it sounds as if Clare's put you on to a good lead but what's it got to do with me?"

"I understand you've got the Warwickshire brigade on his back. I want them called off when he sets out. If he gets a whiff of surveillance, he'll realize we're on to him and take fright. He'll call it off rather than walk into our trap."

"I see what you mean," Brett replied, "but you can forget it. If Garner moves *anywhere*, I'm going to be behind him."

"I'll take responsibility," Jack assured him. "While he's down here in London, we'll keep an eye on him."

"And what if he *is* my kidnapper? He could stop en route to check on his victim. I'm not going to miss that sort of opportunity," Brett replied forcibly.

"This man could be a significant player in art theft. I don't want our operation fouled up."

"Look," Brett hissed down the line, "I have a missing girl and she's worth more than all your precious paintings put together. He *will* be followed every inch of the way by my team. End of argument."

Faced with Brett's passion and obstinacy, Jack relented. "OK, I suppose your case did come first. But make sure your Warwickshire chums do a proper job, won't you? He mustn't know they're tailing him."

"I'll use all the tricks, switching cars, the full works. But he won't stop at a service station for a pee without me knowing about it." Trying to make peace with his London colleague, Brett added, "Thanks for letting me know he's about to leave. I'll get on to Warwickshire straightaway and set up the operation."

He put down the phone and explained the development to Clare and Louise. "Let's not put all our eggs in Garner's basket, though. It's time to interview Ross Mundee again."

"Ah," Clare murmured. "Do I do it on my own or take someone else with me?"

"How about it, Louise?" Brett said to his new recruit. "Part of your training. Go and see a professional like Clare at work."

Louise frowned. "Aren't you going?"

"He can't," Clare put in. "Remember, to Ross Mundee, Brett's a journalist. What if he turns up as a detective now? No problem if Mundee's above board. But," she explained, "if he's our man, he'd realize that Phil and Chloe called us in on Monday night. He'd realize that they disobeyed his first note. He might punish them by punishing Kerry."

"Exactly," Brett said. "Just in case, you'll have to tell him how we got into this – via a witness of the Princess Street crash and subsequent inquiries leading to the Chapmans. You go, Louise, and I'll stay here for this surveillance job, and to tackle anything else that comes in." To Clare he said, "Find out what brand of cigarettes he smokes. You could try and get a sample of his writing as well but he might camouflage it. Still, it's worth it for the ink analysis."

"Brett," Clare cut in firmly, "I realize you're keen

to crack this one, but I do know my job. I don't need instructions."

Brett hesitated and then smiled. "Sorry. You're right. It's just that, when we're dealing with murder victims, time's not so important. They're not under threat any more. But the letter tells us that Kerry's still alive. That means her life's still in danger."

Once he had alerted Warwickshire Constabulary to Garner's impending trip and organized the surveillance, he browsed through Louise's latest additions to the case file. She had not had much luck with customers of the old bike shop but she'd found out a few names of people who had worked there on and off. None of them were known suspects. Even so, Brett would put some of his team on to them, looking for suspicious movements on Monday night and Tuesday morning, for connections to the Chapmans – for anything at all.

Then he went to update the chief. As usual, Big John Macfarlane was in a belligerent mood. "So," he concluded, "you're chasing every bit of forensic evidence that you can scrape together. You and I will never see eye to eye on that one. All those results, they should just confirm what you know by intuition. You leap over intuition to get to the evidence. Waste of energy. Ask Clare. She's a *real* police officer. She understands the criminal brain."

Unwisely, Brett asked, "Then why didn't she—?" He stopped himself making an inappropriate remark in defence of his partner.

"What?"

"Nothing, sir."

Big John stared at him severely and said, "I hope you weren't about to criticize the decision of the selection board. That would be well out of order. But remember, the last round of promotions fell in Keith Johnstone's reign. He was a good but traditional copper. Modern trends passed him by."

Brett assumed that John was referring to the issue of gender in the force.

"What's Clare's view of this case?" the chief enquired.

"You're right. She has her suspicions, unfounded, except on instinct."

"Think about this, Brett. You can't be annoyed on her behalf because some committee's overlooked her and, at the same time, overlook her opinions yourself. She's there to help you lead investigations, not just to follow."

Green team approaching junction thirteen. We're five cars behind target. He's doing eighty-five in the third lane. Are you ready, yellow?

Yeah. Raring to go. Yellow team to Control. You've told Thames Valley cops not to stop him for speeding, haven't you?

Look, you were in nappies when I started doing jobs like this. Just concentrate on driving. Confirm green team to leave motorway at junction thirteen, yellow team to take over.

Sure thing. We're on the slip road, Control. He's just gone past. We'll take up position a good few vehicles behind.

He's way ahead of schedule. If he's supposed to be in north London by five, he's going to be at least an hour early at this rate.

Maybe he wants to case the joint.

Maybe he's just cautious, expecting delays near London.

Maybe he's right. Any congestion ahead, Control?

Nothing spectacular. A bit slow at the roadworks near the end of the motorway. Accident near junction ten, Luton Airport turn, but it's on the northbound carriageway. That's all.

Coming up to junction eleven. Eighty miles an hour, outer lane. Our turn to duck out, Control. Red team in place?

Yes.

Hold it! He's indicating left. This boy's not going to London. He's trying to weave across to the Luton/ Dunstable turning. Oh, no! A lorry's pulling out. Not seen him. He's – Collision in the middle lane! We're braking, Control. His car's rolled. We've got ourselves a pile-up.

Are you OK?

Yeah. But the target's had it, Control. He's not going to walk away from this.

11

"He's what?" Brett exclaimed. In fact, he'd heard exactly what his counterpart in Warwickshire had said into the telephone but Brett did not want to believe it. At twenty-nine minutes past three, Hilary Garner had been killed in a motorway accident. He'd made a hasty change of lanes, apparently in an effort to leave the M1 at the Luton and Dunstable junction, and slammed into the side of a lorry that had pulled out to overtake a slow vehicle. "Why was he turning off?" Brett barked. "Did he see your people and try to lose them?"

"No chance. They were well back. And we swapped cars every two junctions. He couldn't have known we were following him."

"He didn't hear about a hold-up on the radio, did he, and try to find a way round it?"

"Unlikely. All our travel reports told us the south-bound road was more or less clear. And, before you ask, he wasn't distracted by a phone call. We found his mobile in his pocket, not in his hand."

Brett feared the worst. Garner was on his way to London. He would not take a detour without a good reason. It was possible that he had imprisoned Kerry somewhere down south and he intended to see her on his way. Brett closed his eyes and cursed under his breath. With Hilary Garner out of the equation, Kerry would be on her own. At least a live kidnapper would have provided food and water. And he would have led Brett to Kerry. A dead kidnapper could do neither. If Garner was the culprit, his death had put Kerry in even greater peril. She faced a long, slow, solitary degeneration. Brett needed to find some pointers to her whereabouts quickly. Into the phone, he said, "I'll set out as soon as I can. Apply for a warrant, will you? I need to search his house. And I suppose you'd better call Jack Fitzgerald. I'm sure he'll be interested in the contents of our art lover's home."

While Brett hurtled towards Coventry, Clare briefed him about her conversation with Ross Mundee. "He doesn't carry a pen these days, he claims, only a laptop computer. A bit pompous if you ask me. Anyway, it means we wouldn't have got any ink for forensics so I didn't push the hand-writing angle. He's one of those rare people who's ambidextrous. So he said. Louise was quite helpful. She's got a good eye. She watched Mundee and reckoned he was telling the truth. He smoked with both hands. Silk Cut. He picked up a cup of tea with his left hand but, when the phone rang, he answered it with his right. At one point," Clare added, "he took off his specs and went through each pocket, looking for something, a cloth maybe. Then he gave up and cleaned them with a hankie, using his left hand. Louise took it all in." She paused and then continued, "I couldn't get him to admit he'd been near a goat or a bike recently. He said cycling would hardly be the best advert for his trade so he didn't do it. He wouldn't admit to threatening Phil over the hydrogen car either, but he couldn't hide his malice. Clearly, those two are bitter rivals."

"Still on the hit list, then?"

"Definitely."

Louise called to report that the team following up possible sightings of Kerry and Phil's stalker had returned without success. Not one of the leads had shown any promise. And no one on the streets recognized Kerry from her photograph or Phil's stalker from the sketch.

By the time that Brett and Clare reached Coventry, forensic scientists had lifted the wreckage of Hilary Garner's car off the M1 and were beginning to examine it thoroughly under laboratory conditions. Garner's house was buzzing with activity. Local officers were carrying out a routine search for anything that might link Hilary Garner with Kerry Chapman or with another property where he could have abandoned her. Jack Fitzgerald had brought along an art specialist and together they were examining Garner's extensive collection of paintings. Brett was meandering from room to room, hoping to catch sight of something that would provide inspiration. Clare was trying to keep track of both investigations in the same house. Despite her dedication to the kidnap case and her anxiety for Kerry, she could not help being fascinated by the assessment of the works of art.

Jack's sidekick stated, "It's a good find, but not a great find. The Rembrandt and Miro are forgeries, of course. Too much to expect to find the real things. They'd be too expensive for anyone but the mega-rich. These copies are very accomplished, though. I can guess who painted them. Anyway, I bet this Hilary Garner parted with a lot of money for them. But, more importantly, some of the others are genuine. I can think of a couple of galleries who'll be delighted to have some of their stolen pieces back. For example, there's a stolen still life, a delicious bowl of fruit by Ambrosius Bosschaert, early seventeenth century."

Brett's mind wandered. Stolen still life. It reminded him of Kerry. Her normal life had been snatched and suspended until Brett could find her and restore it. He shuddered at the thought. He believed that there was something obvious in this house or among the rest of the evidence that was yelling at him, telling him everything he needed to know to rescue Kerry. Yet somehow, the message was passing him by. He blamed himself for not listening properly.

Clare's mind also drifted, back to the still life hanging in her own front room and to the artist who had painted it for her.

To Jack, Brett said, "Look, what concerns me is Kerry Chapman. Can't you talk to your contacts? On Monday night, was Garner out negotiating a deal on some dodgy painting? If so, where? I need to know."

"I'm not as heartless, not so obsessed with art theft, as you think. I've already got my lads working on it," he replied. Glancing at Clare, he said pointedly, "That's not a sexist comment. I don't have any lasses on the team at the moment. Anyway, they haven't come across any whispers yet."

More conciliatory, Brett replied, "OK, thanks. Let me know if they hear anything, won't you?"

"I can see you're under a lot of pressure. Yes, I will."

Walking round the house with Brett, Clare observed, "It's a long drive from Sheffield to Luton or Dunstable."

"I know," Brett replied. "Something like two or two-and-a-half hours."

"More, if Garner didn't use the motorway," Clare suggested.

"We only checked northbound traffic into Sheffield. He could've gone on the M1 south to the Luton area. More motorway footage to view."

"Anyway," Clare continued, "on Monday night he would've had to lock Kerry into the arch workshop, then drive down and prepare a bolt-hole near Luton. After, he'd probably come back here, home. Early next morning he'd have to drive back to Sheffield, collect Kerry and return to this new lockup. Then finally home. That's a lot of travelling."

"True," Brett agreed. "But not impossible."

"I'm still not convinced."

"Why did he turn off the M1 then?" Brett queried.

Clare shrugged. "Maybe we'll never know. But it's not a crime."

"I wonder." He shouted to one of the local officers, "When Garner crashed, did he have his radio on?"

"Yes," came the reply. "But after the crash it was mangled. Too smashed to work out what he was listening to, I'm told. And it wasn't capable of locking on to police frequencies, if that's what you're thinking."

"That, and something else. What type of radio was it?"

"One of those fancy ones that you can't afford on a police salary. It cuts into whatever you're listening to and gives travel bulletins automatically whenever a radio station puts one out. But the way south was clear."

Brett nodded thoughtfully and continued his tour of the property.

Even after an extensive search, no conclusive evidence emerged. In a notebook, Garner had written Phil Chapman's telephone number at work. But that was hardly surprising. Hilary Garner had admitted that he'd contacted Phil. Brett became more animated when an officer discovered that Garner owned a holiday home, a small thatched cottage in the Lake District. "Thatched," Brett murmured. "We got a bit of straw at Princess Street. That could have come from a thatched roof."

"But," Clare objected, "the Lake District isn't exactly near Luton or Dunstable."

"True," Brett conceded as he dialled Cumbria Constabulary, "but we'll get it checked anyway."

Forty-five minutes later, Brett lost another lead. The Cumbrian police had found that the Lakeland cottage was deserted. By telephone, an officer reported, "We only found one thing of interest. In the basement, there's a large locked trunk. Just in case, we broke into it. It's full of paintings. Classy stuff. Not that I'm any judge."

Brett interrupted. "Hang on. I've got someone here who'll want to speak to you." He yelled for Jack and handed over the phone, saying, "How do you fancy a day in the Lake District? Very nice at this time of year."

The search of the house in Coventry proceeded to its fruitless conclusion. Before Brett set out with

Clare for Sheffield, he asked for all samples of dirt or mud from Garner's shoes and tyres to be sent to Greta. He wanted her to check if they matched the grime in the Sheffield workshop or the soil in the wood. He also arranged for samples of Hilary Garner's writing to be examined by George.

"I know I should be thinking about Garner," Clare said as she stood by Miro's Crying Lady, "but I've just had a thought about Phil's stalker."

"Oh?" Brett prompted. He recalled Big John's advice not to overlook her instinct.

"Yesterday we agreed she might've stopped plaguing Phil because she's taken Kerry. But you'd have to ask, why Kerry and why now? I may be way off the mark, but there could be a reason. On Monday, Phil said this woman had been obsessed with him for nine months. What if she felt she'd been 'going out' with him for nine months? Interestingly, the length of a pregnancy. She might want to seal the imagined relationship with a child, conceived, in her mind, when they first met. Perhaps she wants – she expects – his child. She might be 'mothering' Kerry to make her feel closer to Phil, to make her feel like his wife."

Brett contemplated it. He took it seriously, or as seriously as his scientific mind allowed. "Right now, we can use all the ideas we can get, even if they're far-fetched."

Clare snorted. "I suppose you have to hold the rank of inspector before you can come up with sensible theories."

"Come on, Clare. You know I didn't mean it like that. Sure, I'm supposed to be big on ideas, but you know as well as I do that it's usually me that gets criticized for being too elaborate."

Sulkily, she said, "Like this far-fetched idea about an art collector driving all over the place to collect a child as well."

"You might be right," Brett replied. "Look," he said quietly to her, "I know it's bugging you but remember I wasn't the one who turned down your promotion."

He was right, of course. But he was also part of the big boys' club now, part of the system. Clare resented that system, not Brett. She gave so much of herself to the police force, she had been injured so many times and would probably be injured again, she had sacrificed relationships for her work, and the system had still shut the door on her. She loved her profession, the satisfaction of apprehending the bad guys, but she believed that sometimes it should acknowledge the demands that it made and reward her.

Brett said, "We've got to move fast, for Kerry's sake. We need to find out if there's more in your stalker idea than pseudo-psychology and speculation."

Clare interrupted. "You think all psychology's pseudo-psychology." Disgruntled, she added, "All that info I gave you last night on stalkers was real. What I've just said fits in with it."

"I know," he replied. "I just need something more solid. It's the way I am." The tension was getting to them all. It had nearly driven Phil and Chloe apart. Now, it was doing much the same to Brett and Clare. Usually, the difference between them was a strength but this time it was becoming a matter of contention. "We need facts about her. But how? We haven't had any leads so far." Brett paused and then murmured, "Chloe reckoned the stalking started after Phil's TV appearance on some pollution debate."

"Yes," Clare confirmed. "His stalker was probably watching."

"We all take a passing fancy to someone we see on the box, but falling in love via the screen? Unlikely." Abruptly, Brett realized, "There are two ways of watching – not just one! I wonder if she saw him in the flesh." Immediately Brett called Phil and asked, "That TV debate. Was there a studio audience?"

"Yes," Phil replied. "An invited audience from various interest groups. Why?"

"I just find it more believable that your stalker got hooked on you if she saw you for real. Did you notice her in the audience?"

"Not that I remember. It was just a small sea of faces to me."

Next, Brett phoned Louise. "Something important's cropped up," he told her. "A fresh line of inquiry."

"So you found something at Garner's place?" Louise asked excitedly.

"Not really. This is altogether different. Call the television company that put together Phil's debate on pollution nine months ago, Yorkshire TV. See if they've still got a list of the studio audience. If they have, get all the female names, please. And," Brett added, "there is a bit of trawling you can do to help with the Garner line. Check with all local radio stations – local to Luton and thereabouts, that is – for any travel news they broadcast at three-thirty, the time of the crash. Transcripts of anything that went out between three o'clock and half past would be helpful. Thanks, Louise. Keep up the good work." He put the phone back in his pocket, looked at his partner and said, "Of course, there's a problem with the stalker idea."

"What's that?" Clare asked defensively.

"Kerry's letter. Phil's got to come to his senses and give up something. It still sounds like his hydrogen secrets," Brett reasoned. "It doesn't sound like a message from a deranged stalker."

"I wouldn't be so sure," Clare said. "She might be talking about Chloe."

12

At seven o'clock Brett and Clare were taking a break from driving, sipping hot watery coffee at a service station, when Louise called back.

"I got hold of the programme researcher pretty easily," she reported, "but she didn't keep a list of the audience. All she remembers is contacting different groups, to get a balanced audience, she said." Reading from her notes, Louise recounted, "She invited people from the RAC and the AA, Friends of the Earth, the Road Hauliers' Association, Sheffield Cycle Club, the science and technology faculties of local universities, the Health and Safety Executive, and the Asthma Association." She hesitated before adding, "And Morlands and Sabre Cars."

"Interesting," Brett murmured. "Thanks. It's important that I take it on from here."

At the other end of the line, an embarrassed Louise replied, "I've got contact numbers for all those we don't know already and I ... er..."

"What?" Brett put down his mug of coffee.

"I'm sorry but I've called the universities and HSE already," she confessed. "I thought you'd want me to find out if anyone went along to the programme." With a quaking voice, she said, "I didn't know you'd want to do it yourself."

"Never mind," Brett replied, endeavouring to reassure his assistant. Internally, though, he was annoyed. First, he'd almost squabbled with Clare. Now, Louise may have alerted Phil's stalker and Kerry's kidnapper to their progress by making contact with the interest groups. Brett didn't want to dampen Louise's initiative but she could have jeopardized the case, or Kerry. "It's done now so forget it," Brett said, with all the sincerity that he could muster. Adapting his tone to avoid denting Louise's growing confidence, he added, "Crack on with the radio travel news instead and leave the rest of those groups to us. It'll need a deft touch."

"Sorry," Louise repeated.

"As you looked into it, aren't you going to tell me what you found out?" Brett prompted. "*Did* you find out if anyone from the universities or the HSE went?"

Downhearted, she answered, "Two from the HSE and one from Sheffield Hallam University. All men. And one from the University of Sheffield but

I don't know if it's a man or a woman."

"What's this person's name?"

"They had to spell it for me, you know. I'm not sure how you say it." Stuttering, she pronounced, "Naoki Matsumoto."

"Professor Matsumoto," Brett said. "Well, well, well. He didn't mention it to us. I wonder if it's relevant."

Finally, Louise remarked, "Those radio stations in the Midlands and the south, I'm having trouble with them. Not very co-operative, you know. Sorry."

"Keep on at them till you get what I want. Don't take no for an answer."

Brett and Clare finished their drinks and once again joined the northbound traffic on the M1. "Are you getting a meal when we get back?" asked Brett. He was hoping that they could patch up their partnership over dinner.

Clare shrugged. "I was supposed to meet some mates tonight. Out celebrating a friend's birthday."

"Sorry," Brett said.

"They're used to me not turning up. A social life and police work don't mix." Ruefully, she added, "All my socializing is with police officers, and crooks. So, if you're inviting me out for a bite, the answer's yes."

"I know what you mean. I said I'd go to midweek rugby training," Brett declared. "But, same here. I lost my place on the team some time ago. Lack of commitment. I still turn up for training when I can, which is hardly ever during a case. Especially this one. I can't help thinking of Kerry, locked away, maybe without water." Suddenly depressed, he looked at Clare glumly and said, "Do you know how long a human being can last without water? Especially in hot weather."

His concern for his goddaughter touched Clare. She answered, "Not long, but she might have water, Brett. Lots of it." Keeping her eyes on the road, she added, "She might be getting more food than we do. We don't know."

"Yeah. But..." His voice drowned in frustration and the burden of responsibility.

Clare glanced at him and observed, "You're scared in case you let her down."

"You know my family background," he said. The drone of the car made his voice seem like an intimate whisper. "Not much of a family at all. So I invested in Kerry, I suppose." He sighed loudly. "I used to play football with her, take her swimming and skating sometimes. Skating's not one of my favourite occupations but she loved it. She was pretty good. Better than me." He smiled at the memory. "She even came to see me play rugby. Yes, I'm worried about her, worried that I won't be able to get to her in time."

"You're doing all you can," Clare stressed. "You don't let anyone down if you do your best. You can't do any more."

"You know the problem, don't you?" Brett said. "We've got lots of little isolated facts and no link between them. The jacket with chalk, the code number, the arch workshop, the notes, the spelling mistake. Where's the big idea that links them?" Brett did not expect an answer. He regarded it as his job to come up with the big ideas. That was supposed to be one of his strengths. He shook his head glumly.

Back at headquarters, the incident room was quiet. Only Louise remained obstinately at her post. "Still trying radio stations," she reported. "I've got a few faxed travel updates but nothing looks, you know, important. I'm still trying Three Counties Radio. At least they're staffed at night. Someone who's just come on night duty might have the time to help, they said. And," Louise added, "Greta mailed you some stuff before she left. Want to see?"

"Definitely," Brett answered, bending down towards the monitor as Louise clicked on the forensic folder. The cigarette stubs in the Princess Street workshop were Superkings and Silk Cut. No lipstick stains. The pieces of broken glass were unexceptional. They could have come from a tumbler, beer glass, vase, almost anything. The team had not found any blood but there were plenty of fingerprints. Some matched with perpetrators of petty crime, mostly theft. A few partial prints in the dust were almost certainly Kerry's. The dart flight bore two clear fingerprints, so Brett left a request for someone to take Alan Fox's prints for cross-referencing. Two strands of hair matched Kerry's taken from her comb. The dried mud revealed little but it contained two small pebbles of dolomite.

"What's dolomite?" Clare queried.

Brett answered, "It's a rock, and a mineral. I can't remember what it is chemically. Like limestone, I think."

Some shoe impressions were Kerry's size and the rest were mainly from trainers of various sizes. There were traces of nicotine on the lens cloth so, Brett deduced, it had been used by a smoker. The ink used in Kerry's letter was identical to that of the kidnap note. The only fingerprints on the paper were very faint and probably Kerry's. The ones on the envelope belonged to the postman. A small round patch near the bottom of the sheet bore the residue of a teardrop. Analysis by ESDA revealed some of the words from the kidnapper's first message, proving that the new letter had been written on the next page of the pad. According to Greta's summary, there was a faint smear of blue dye, invisible to the naked eye, in the bottom right-hand corner of the letter. A trace of formaldehyde came from the same area of the paper.

"What's formaldehyde?"

"It's a disinfectant," Brett answered. "Very powerful. It's used as a solution called formalin, dyed blue for safety, so it's easily seen."

"So, someone's cleaned up the place before they put Kerry in it. Very thoughtful," Clare replied cynically.

"More than likely," Brett muttered. "But what we're getting is more bits and pieces. Still no big picture."

Clare grabbed her partner's arm and tugged on it, saying, "Come on. I'm taking you to the health club. You need a break. So do I. It's getting on top of us, this case, and making us feel low. A swim followed by a jacuzzi should do it."

Resisting, Brett objected, "Not while Kerry's—"

"I'm thinking of us *and* Kerry. If there's a big picture to see, we're more likely to see it when we're relaxed. And then there's that meal you almost promised me."

Louise nodded and smiled. "I'll mind the shop," she volunteered.

Brett's big muscular body was not really built for swimming. He lacked the suppleness required to be really good. His natural power pulled him through the water clumsily but fast. Clare's strength and agility gave her a more elegant, proficient and impressive style. Brett rested after several lengths at speed. He felt some muscles, not heavily stretched by running, squash or rugby, begin to ache. It was a pleasant ache, reminding him that he should swim more often. For a while, he watched appreciatively as Clare carved a path through the water with a refined backstroke and then front crawl, barely making a splash. She was an excellent partner, in all sorts of ways. He did not want a rift to open up between them. He needed her.

Along the left-hand side of the pool there was an extended window. On the other side of the glass, fitness fanatics were working out in the gym, testing themselves against the exercise equipment, straining every sinew. The collection of contraptions made the room look like a torture chamber. Several of the tortured specimens in the sweat-filled gym were probably Clare's mates. Perhaps they were wondering who Brett was, assuming that he was her new boyfriend.

Clare pulled up beside him, ran her hands through her hair and said, "Feeling better?"

"I suppose so. Even if a bit guilty. Phil and Chloe won't be feeling this good."

"Jacuzzi?"

Brett nodded and followed her.

In the hot bubbling tub Brett felt like a vegetable simmering in a pot. Pummelled from all sides, it was a pleasurable all-over massage. Clare reclined opposite him. All he could see of her was her shoulders, neck, face and flattened red hair. Her shoulders had been reddened by the sun and her nose was showing the first signs of peeling. Underwater, their legs and feet tangled occasionally. For the first time since Monday evening, they pondered things other than Kerry and art theft. The gym,

Clare's friends, the choosing of a restaurant for their dinner. Brett began to feel like a normal human being again.

Suddenly, at the side of the cauldron, Louise appeared. Embarrassed, she coughed to gain their attention. Her uncertain and apologetic expression told them that she was not sure whether she should be disturbing them. She was clothed but had removed her shoes to walk by the pool. She squatted down with a couple of papers in her hand, and announced, "Sorry to bother you, but I thought you might want to hear this straightaway. A fix on those travel updates from local radio stations down south."

All notion of being a normal person vanished. No one normal was briefed by an assistant while lazing in a jacuzzi. "Yes? Let's hear it," Brett urged.

"I think you'll be interested in two of them," Louise said, blushing. "At three twenty-eight – less than a minute before Garner crashed – this went out." She read from a fax transmission, "News just coming in of an accident on the M1 at junction ten. All you southbound M1 surfers would do well to avoid it. You'll get more news first on this station, as soon as we get it."

In his eagerness, Brett was tempted to cut in with a question but he forced himself to keep quiet and let Louise finish her story.

"This one," she said, waving a second fax, "was broadcast four minutes later. Just after Garner crashed." Scanning the piece of paper, she said, "We've got more details for you on that M1 incident. Apparently, you're in the clear if you're southbound. We've just had it confirmed that it's beyond junction ten on the *northbound* carriageway. A transporter has shed its load of cars over all three lanes. Bad news. You can't even pick up a brand new car as you'll be diverted off the motorway at junction ten." She looked up at Brett and said, "I thought you'd want to know."

"You were right," he replied. "Very right." Encouraging her, he asked, "What have you deduced?"

Louise replied, "Garner heard that the M1 was blocked at junction ten when he was coming up to junction eleven. I looked at a road atlas. You know, there's a way to avoid junction ten by going off at junction eleven, through Dunstable, and getting back on the motorway at junction nine. Perhaps that's what he tried to do. He made a split-second decision to leave the motorway and avoid a hold-up that didn't exist."

Brett was nodding. "And instead, caused one himself."

"Yes," Louise agreed.

Clare interjected, "No evidence for him visiting Kerry en route, then."

"That's right. Garner might have just lost his position as chief suspect," Brett said. "Thanks, Louise. You were right to come. Good detective work at HQ, and in finding us here. Remind me to request a doubling of your attachment period."

Looking relieved, Louise beamed.

"After that, you deserve a break as well. Knock off for the night," Brett suggested. "Why don't you hang on for a bit and come with us for a bite to eat?"

Clare nodded. "Good idea."

Abashed, Louise said, "No, thanks. I couldn't."

"OK," Brett replied. "It's up to you. Another time, maybe."

Louise nodded, got up and stretched.

"Thanks again."

As soon as the poolside door closed behind her, Clare chuckled.

"What's up with you?" asked Brett.

"She was scared of playing gooseberry! I think I know what she reckons we get up to out of hours."

Brett smiled. "Yeah." Keen to change the subject, he said, "But she's good. I wish we could keep her, no matter what she thinks about you and me." He inclined his head towards the gym and commented, "I've never understood the people who cycle on those exercise bikes. Why don't they get a real bike and go out in the hills? Much nicer way of exercising."

Clare grinned. "It doesn't rain inside. And you don't get punctures."

At once, Brett leapt out of the swirling water. "That's it! You're brilliant, Clare."

"I am?" she queried, still simmering in the jacuzzi.

"Time to go," Brett decided. "We've got work to
do."

I t was a warm and muggy night. The obstinate
hours of daylight had not quite succumbed to the
dark. Clare drove the short distance to the city
centre with her hair still wet from swimming. She
dropped down into second gear to turn left and her
exhaust belched pollution. To Brett, she objected,
"The shop'll be closed at this time of night. Just
about the only places that'll be open are pubs, clubs
and restaurants, hint, hint."

Determined, Brett tapped the pocket where he
kept his mobile phone and said, "I've arranged to
have it opened especially for us. I called Control
from the changing room. They're contacting the
owner."

"Makes you wonder how we managed before
mobile phones."

They parked on double-yellow lines outside the bicycle shop and peered into the darkened interior. They could just make out racks of bikes and shelves of accessories.

"Looks like we're first here," Clare remarked. She believed that, in his current mood, Brett might just break into the shop without waiting for the manager. He was pacing up and down restlessly outside and in the gloom, the occasional passer-by glanced at him furtively. Within five minutes, a squad car pulled up and two uniformed officers jumped out, eager to question two potential burglars committing a traffic offence. Clare smiled at the irony and extracted her warrant card. The constables took one look at her ID, apologized and explained that she and Brett were within camera shot of the city centre's closed-circuit television system. One of them gestured towards the camera, mounted high on a building across the road. The security company had alerted the police to two suspicious characters loitering outside the shop.

As soon as the police car had accelerated away, it was replaced by the manager's. Looking crabby, he came up to them, introduced himself as Tony, and unlocked the shop. "For the first time," he moaned, "I wish someone had gone to the competition on the other side of town rather than choose me." He sighed and said, "Come in. I'll turn the alarm off and the lights on."

By the time that the strip lights had settled to a

steady blaze, Brett already had a puncture-repair kit in his hand. For Clare's benefit, he recited the contents list from the front of the box. "Includes adhesive, marker crayon, feather edge patches, *chalk*, sandpaper." Brett looked up. "I remember fixing punctures. After sticking the patch on, you scatter chalk around it to soak up the excess glue."

Clare nodded significantly.

From the row of cycles, Brett asked Tony, "Do you stock lots of makes?"

Still frowning, the manager replied, "Quite a few of the market leaders. Apollo, Raleigh and so on." He hurtled towards the front door where some boys were about to stroll in.

While Tony explained to the inquisitive lads that his shop was really closed, Brett ambled along the line of cycles, which were mostly mountain bikes. When Tony returned, Brett enquired, "Is there an identifying mark on each bike? A sort of serial number?"

"A frame number," Tony replied. "Underneath. Stamped under the bottom bracket."

Brett nodded thoughtfully. "And how about Peugeot? Do they make bikes as well as cars?"

"Yes. Peugeot Cycles. They're not so fashionable now. These days they tend to supply basic parts to other companies rather than make bikes under their own brand name. I don't keep new Peugeots but I've got a second-hand one, a man's racing bike, out the back."

"Let's take a look," Brett said.

Brett ignored Tony's grumbling as he led them into the workshop and turned on the light. Among the bicycle jungle there was a lightweight racing bike with "Peugeot" emblazoned along the crossbar and the lion logo printed on both front forks. Brett tipped up the bike and examined it underneath.

"There it is," Tony said, pointing to the frame number below the crank.

Brett read aloud, "02213498."

Tony gazed accusingly at Clare and then at Brett. "Are you saying it's been stolen? Is that what it's all about? All this fuss for one nicked bike?"

"No," Clare answered. "We don't care about this particular bike. But it's told us a lot about another one, and about a missing child. Have you sold any other Peugeots recently?"

"No."

"Tell me," Clare continued, "does your competitor, the other cycle shop, sell second-hand bikes like this one?"

"Yes. Not openly, but it does."

She smiled at Tony and said, "Thanks. You've been very useful. You can shut up shop now."

Brett was on the phone as soon as he climbed into the car. To Control, he said forcefully, "I don't care if he's in bed, down at the pub, in hospital, visiting his mum. Just contact the owner, or any member of staff, and get him or her to meet us at the shop. If no one comes, Clare'll use her credit card, or I'll use a shoulder, to get us in. One way or the other, I'm going to inspect the bikes in that shop."

The swoop on the second cycle shop turned out to be unhelpful. Only one of the bikes was a Peugeot and its frame number was not 01203775. Like Tony, the owner, a Mrs Keane, denied handling any other racing cycles made by Peugeot. Brett and Clare learned nothing more from Mrs Keane and gave up the chase for the evening. Instead, they had a long-awaited late-night dinner in the city centre.

"So," Clare said over her plate of spare ribs, "cycling's the key. The big idea. The chalk might have come from someone who'd fixed a puncture. And someone with a puncture-repair kit might've known about the disused bike workshop. There's something else that fits," she deduced. "The person who wrote the first kidnap message had probably jotted down the make and frame number of a bike on the page above. But why?"

It was easy for Brett to imagine someone scribbling down a bicycle's details, perhaps while on the phone, perhaps while in a second-hand shop, perhaps in the arch workshop. It was much more difficult to decide who had made the note and why. "I don't know," he confessed. "But I know why Louise didn't crack the code. It's not her fault. When she called Peugeot, she only spoke to the car division. Pity. At least I'm happier with the case. We've got a bike theory. That gives us something to shoot at, to prove or disprove. Tomorrow we start."

"Where?"

"Links. We start with one of those telephone numbers Louise got for us. Remember? She said the Sheffield Cycling Club had been invited to Phil's TV debate. Maybe there's a connection. After this, though," Brett said, pointing with a fork at his salad, "I'm going to Phil and Chloe's. At least I can be a bit more upbeat for them tonight."

It was three in the morning and Brett had come and gone. Phil and Chloe were still sitting up, not daring to move far from the telephone. The night was eerie, close and airless. Two small beads of sweat rolled down Phil's brow and the back of his shirt was wet. It wasn't just the heat.

In the last three days they'd gone through hell. At first they'd supported each other in their mutual grief and worry. Then, unable to lash out at the real culprit, they'd taken it out on each other. In particular, Chloe blamed Phil for their daughter's disappearance. Now, since the arrival of Kerry's letter, a numbness, a feeling of helplessness, had set in. It did not diminish their anger. Because the numbness did not provide an outlet for their wrath, their hurt was internalized and amplified. They lived in an unbearable, vacuous limbo. They were not capable of settling down to anything: food, sleep, exercise, housework. It all seemed so unimportant. They felt hungry but too sickened to eat. They felt hot and sticky but too distracted to take a shower. They were exhausted but too highly strung to sleep.

"Even in the middle of the night, when she'd be tucked up in bed," Chloe muttered, "I miss her. I can sense she's not up there. The house seems empty. It's awful."

"Incomplete," Phil added.

Chloe glanced at her husband. Even in the dark, she could tell that he was weeping silently. She couldn't remember ever seeing him cry before. "You're saying that whoever's got Kerry is winning. They wanted us to know what it's like, being incomplete, and now we do."

"But we've got Brett on our side," Phil said in desperation. "We couldn't ask for anyone better. He's my friend. He'll get her back. That's all I care about."

"I hope so," Chloe said. After a few quiet seconds, she added, "But he hasn't had much success, has he?"

Phil sighed and wiped his eyes. "At least he knows he's looking for a cyclist now." Said aloud, it sounded meagre, pathetic even.

"You've got a lot of faith in him," Chloe observed.

"Do you remember when Kerry broke her arm tobogganing down Abbey Lane Golf Course? We set off up the hill at the same time, you, me and Brett. I've never seen anything like it. Brett easily beat us to her and carried her down like she weighed nothing. The roads were jammed but, on the way to the hospital, he radioed ahead and got the traffic cops to clear the way for us. He got into trouble for that, you know. Misuse of his position." Phil swallowed but the lump in his throat remained. "He'll find her."

Chloe buried her head in her arms. In a muffled voice, she said, "I hope you're right. And I hope he's not too late when he does." She dissolved in tears.

Any notion of Hilary Garner's involvement in Kerry's kidnap evaporated on Thursday morning. Videos taken on the M1 near Luton had captured Garner's Ventura heading towards London on Monday afternoon. Also, Jack Fitzgerald called to report that one of his informants had divulged that a Midlands businessman had been acquiring a few pieces recently. "The word is that this man's been sold a few dummies as well as some of the genuine articles. It sounds very much like Hilary Garner. I heard he was fishing around in London early on Monday evening."

Brett thanked the art specialist and crossed Hilary Garner off his list of suspects. Garner had faked a migraine and lied about his movements to conceal his dealing in stolen paintings. He had not stolen Kerry. Brett called Greta to cancel the analysis of mud from Garner's shoes and tyres. Knowing that Alan Fox was a cyclist and a dart player whose alibi was not foolproof, Brett also asked Greta to prioritize the work on his prints and the dart flight. Then Brett enjoyed telling George that his opinions on Garner's handwriting were now superfluous.

Louise had got two phone numbers for Sheffield Cycling Club, one for the secretary and one for the chairman. Brett did not get a response from the first number so he tried the second. It was answered by Roland Barnes, the chairman. When Brett asked about the environmental discussion on television, Roland remembered it. "The television people called Sophie, our secretary," he said. "I seem to remember she got a couple of our members interested in going but I don't know who. You'd have to speak to her."

"Sophie who?"

"Dyer. Sophie Dyer."

Brett took down her details and then asked, "Do you have any members with Peugeot bikes, or who deal with them?"

Roland thought. "Not especially. But someone might have one. I don't know everyone's bikes."

"Do you keep a list of the bikes your members own?"

"No. We're a club, not Big Brother," answered Roland. "I'll tell you what we do keep: a list of all bikes that get stolen. If a member, or anyone else in Sheffield, has their cycle stolen, they can tell us and we keep a note of it. We call the list ROBS – Registry of Bikes Stolen. We send it out to local bike shops so that when they're offered bikes for sale or exchange, they can check them against ROBS, to see if they've been stolen. We've got a few bikes back that way. It's more than the police manage, if you'll allow me to say so. Perhaps you're too busy to chase bike thefts."

Ignoring the criticism, Brett enquired quickly, "How do you identify the missing bikes?"

"Make, colour, any uncommon features, and frame number."

"Interesting." Brett sat bolt upright with a tingling in his spine. "Who keeps this list? You?"

"I've got an abbreviated version of the list. The full details are administered by Sophie."

If he had not been on the phone and at a delicate stage of the conversation, Brett would have punched the air and cried out, "Yes!" Instead, he kept calm and asked, "Can you look on the list, please, and tell me if there's a Peugeot on it, frame number 01203775."

"Just a second. I'll get it. You'd be amazed how many bikes go walkies."

"I'll hold," Brett said. He tapped a biro on the desk while he waited. With a hand over the mouthpiece, he muttered, "Come on, come on."

Eventually, Roland picked up the receiver again.

"Yes," he informed Brett. "A bike with that frame number's on ROBS. It disappeared just last week, in fact. But it's not a Peugeot. That's all I know. If you need any more information, you'll have to talk to Sophie about it."

"Do you know where she is right now?"

"I'm the chairman, not Big Brother," Roland replied, repeating what seemed to be his favourite saying. "But perhaps she's at work."

"Where's that?"

"Doncaster. She works at Beaches, the travel agent."

"And is it true that all details of missing bikes would be phoned to her by the people who have them stolen?" Brett queried.

"No, it wouldn't. A lot are, but sometimes she'll get a note written by the unfortunate cyclist. It might be posted or given to her by hand at a meeting."

"And if I want a list of your members?"

"Sophie," the chairman replied curtly. "I don't have one."

"Does the name Alan Fox ring a bell?"

"I can't say it does, no. But I don't know all our members by name, if that's what you're getting at."

"OK, thanks a lot," Brett concluded. He put down the phone, stood up and declared to the room, "Now we're getting somewhere! Time to move into top gear." He briefed the team and said urgently, "All efforts to be put into Sheffield Cycling Club and its members. Forget Ventura phone numbers for the moment. We need to speak to Sophie Dyer, desperately. That falls to me and Clare. We need someone out talking to Alan Fox. I guess he'll be at Morlands. I know he's not left-handed but he *is* a cyclist who had a puncture on Monday night, just before Kerry was kidnapped. Is he a member of this cycling club? He was riding a new bike, he told me, so he might have just had one nicked. Did he, or anyone else, report a stolen bike to Sheffield Cycling Club or to us? Louise, check all South Yorkshire records. Remember, the two people most likely to write 01203775 on a piece of paper are Sophie Dyer and the previous owner of the bike. They're top of our list."

While Clare listened to Brett, she applied a liberal layer of sun screen to her face, neck and bare arms. She was anticipating another scorcher. She was also contemplating the authority in her partner's manner, so different from his first unsure steps of a year ago. Then, he was a minor player in John Macfarlane's team, a schoolboy signing. To John and most of the others he'd been an unwelcome disruption to the game plan. But he had turned out to be a star striker. Now, he dished out the orders and his team responded to his emotionally charged state. Clare could tell that they respected him. As for herself, she distrusted her feelings towards him. In the Messenger case, she'd seen him at his most vulnerable when he'd had to face his own uncom-fortable past and she'd seen him at his most courageous when he'd rescued his parents. She'd also seen him at his lowest point, when he blamed himself for his girlfriend's murder, and she'd seen him at his best, surrounded by bewildering facts and embroidering them cleverly into credible theories. Clare did not entirely trust her feelings because it was easy to confuse shared experiences with attachment.

"Should I phone Beaches?" Louise piped up. "You know, to see if Sophie Dyer's there?"

"No," answered Brett. "I'm going anyway. If she's there we'll take her by surprise. If she's not we'll ask around about her. You work on identifying the owner of that missing bike. I want two people outside Dyer's house, and a call from them as soon as she shows up." Turning to Louise again, Brett said, "Get a video of that TV programme as well. Let's print out stills of any audience shots and see if we can spot anyone we know. Remember, every-one," he boomed, "there's a seven-year-old relying on us. I want to arrest a kidnapper, not a murderer. Let's get going."

The travel agent's was crushed between a betting shop, pompously proclaiming itself to be a turf accountant, and the local branch of Waters Pharmacy. Clare was tempted to comment that Beaches was fittingly situated between turf and water but she recognized that Brett was not in the mood for humour. They strode directly into the travel agency, which was long and narrow, like a beach. Three young women were sitting in a line at their stations. Each had the standard equipment of a computer, a phone, a pen, a Beaches T-shirt and a smile. Two of the three were occupied with customers, arranging a late booking and a Christmas break overseas. The third woman was sifting hurriedly through next year's brochures. She wore a badge that identified her as Kara, the manager of the agency. With the air of the head girl at school, she looked up at the police officers and said, "Can I help you?"

Taking the lead, Clare introduced herself and Brett. When she asked if Sophie was on duty, Kara answered, "No, she's off this week: holiday."

"Where's she gone? Did she say?"

"Yeah. She said she wasn't going anywhere. Staying at home to get stuff done around the house."

Clare showed her the sketch of Phil's stalker and asked, "Is this Sophie?"

Kara studied the likeness and shrugged. "It's *like* her. That's all."

Brett's phone rang and, while Clare carried on with the interview, Brett wandered to the quiet end of the room to listen to the news from Louise.

"The officers you sent to Alan Fox," she began. "I've just heard from them. He told them he isn't a member of Sheffield Cycle Club and he hasn't had a bike nicked. He said he bought a new one just because he fancied it. And no one reported the missing bike to us, either, by the way. But there *is* something else you might be interested in. At Morlands, Fox works with a chap called Ed Tarrant – to be precise, Edward O Tarrant or EOT. And he's left-handed."

"Ed," Brett murmured. "I saw him. A darts player."

"That reminds me. Greta says the dabs on the dart flight aren't Alan Fox's."

"Let's get Ed Tarrant's, then. See if they're his. When I saw him, someone said he was burgled last week. Check if he lost a bike. You know the frame number. What about news from Sophie's house?" Brett queried.

"Nothing. We've got two people outside but the place is deserted," Louise answered.

"Damn!" he muttered under his breath. Then he continued, "There's something I need, Louise. A search warrant to get in there and take a look around. In particular, I need a photo of her. Start an application to the magistrate, will you? I'll approve it when I get back."

"But—"

"Don't tell me. You haven't done it before."

"Sorry," Louise replied plaintively.

"All right. Talk to someone in the team who has. No time like the present for learning." He rang off and went back to the conversation with Kara.

For Brett's benefit, Clare repeated an answer that Kara had just given. "So, Sophie's a left-hander." Then she asked, "Is she single, married?"

"Single."

"Boyfriend?" Clare enquired.

"She mentions a man now and again," Kara responded. "In fact," she sighed and added, "quite a lot, actually. It gets a bit tedious. No man can be as good as she claims hers is. Seems to spend a lot of time with him. Name of Phil."

Clare and Brett exchanged a glance.

"Do you know his surname?"

"No, she never mentions it. And we don't ask. If we expressed an interest, she'd take it as encouragement to lecture us silly. You see, she either doesn't say a word or she chatters all the time. With Sophie there's no middle ground." Kara paused before adding, "Sometimes she lectures us about the joys of cycling instead."

"She cycles a lot?"

"She runs some cycling club. Even comes to work on a bike in good weather. That's a good few miles."

"And in bad weather?" Clare queried.

"She's got a car. An old white Escort."

"Is Sophie good at her job?" Clare asked delicately.

"Well," Kara answered hesitantly, "could do better, to be honest. I hope I'm not getting her into trouble. I've already said her social skills are iffy. You see, she's not comfortable enough in front of customers. She's a bit odd, actually. She's clever and competent but she doesn't get on with people very well. And that's essential in this job."

Brett put in, "We've got information that Sophie's not at home but we really need to speak to her. It's *very* important. Obviously, she knows the travel business. Maybe she booked herself a little retreat somewhere through Beaches. Can you check?"

"Sure," Kara answered, gazing appreciatively at Brett. "If she did, it'll be on the computer. Just give me a second."

While Kara clattered the keys and glanced occasionally at her monitor, Brett said in a quiet voice to Clare, "It's too easy. *If* she's got Kerry and if she booked a place to stay from here, I bet she wouldn't use her real name."

Kara looked up and said, "No. There's nothing, I'm afraid."

Clare thought about it for a moment and then suggested, "Try Sophie Chapman."

Brett nodded. "Brilliant idea. Go for it."

And yet, after an agonizingly long thirty seconds, Kara still found nothing.

"How about Kerry Chapman?" Clare asked, persevering with her line of reasoning.

Eventually, Kara stopped typing and shook her head. There was no record at Beaches of Sophie arranging a get-away-from-it-all holiday for herself and a bogus daughter.

Continuing the interview, Clare enquired, "Have you got an example of Sophie's writing?"

Kara shrugged. "I suppose so. Somewhere. We

all scribble down lots of notes while we're on the phone but, when we've got a deal sorted out, all the important stuff goes on to the computer. Notes go into the bin. You want me to look around anyway?"

"Please."

Kara's search was futile and she apologized for her failure.

"Thanks anyway," Clare said. Before leaving, she gave Kara her telephone number. "Give me a call if she turns up, or if you come across her writing – or anything else that'll help us to find her."

In the car, Brett said, "It's not certain yet. Not by any means. We've got Sophie Dyer and the kidnapper, separated by a stepping stone. The stepping stone's Phil's stalker. If Dyer *is* the kidnapper, we've got to confirm she's the stalker and then prove that the stalker's the kidnapper. Sophie's a hot candidate for Phil's stalker. She's certainly obsessed with someone called Phil. We need to get a photo of her and show it to Phil. That'll confirm the first step, or disprove it. Second, Sophie may have written down the ID on the missing bike for Sheffield Cycling Club, and George thinks the same hand wrote the kidnap note. But we've got to work on that. The second step's far from wrapped up yet. There's an Edward Tarrant who works alongside Alan Fox at Morlands. He's left-handed, his initials are EOT and he's been burgled recently. Coincidence? Did he lose a bike in the burglary? That would explain the EOT written by the frame number now that it can't be the end of Peugeot. If Tarrant's in the cycling club, he could have jotted it down and given it to a perfectly innocent Sophie Dyer."

"We need Sophie and her ROBS list," Clare concluded.

Brett struck the top of the dashboard with his fist. "Where the hell is she?"

Back in the incident room, Louise looked at him sheepishly. She had prepared the documentation for the application of a search warrant and it needed only Brett's signature, but she had bad news. She had learned that there would be a delay of a few hours in the busy magistrate's office.

Brett cursed. Making up his mind, he said, "OK, push it through the system, Louise, but I'm going in as soon as we get there."

Clare argued, "We haven't got grounds for entry and search without a warrant, Brett."

"We have. I'm authorizing it to save life or prevent serious injury to Kerry."

"But," Clare objected, "you know as well as I do, you'd have to reasonably believe Kerry was on the premises to make those grounds stick."

"I do," Brett insisted with a determined grin. "But if she isn't, we'll just take a look at the ROBS list and seize a photograph. That's all. A full search can wait for the warrant."

"Big John'll have something to say about it," Clare

remarked.

"True," Brett replied. "But not till after I've got what I want." Before they headed back towards their car, Brett said to Louise, "Something else for you. Dyer's got a white Escort. Trace its registration and put out a call for it. But no approach. If someone spots it, get on to me."

Brett bent down to the car window and asked his officers outside Sophie's house, "Still nothing?"

"We've seen more action in Highfield cemetery," a bored constable replied.

"Or in the goal mouth that the Blades are attacking," his colleague added.

Brett smiled and said, "Thanks. We're going in. Let me know if anything happens out here."

It was a small house near the top of a long, old brick-built terrace that plunged down the steep narrow street. At the door, Brett banged vainly with the knocker. After a few seconds he glanced at Clare and commented, "More subtlety called for." He picked up a brick from the tiny front garden and smashed the pane of frosted glass in the door.

As Brett pushed his hand carefully through the jagged hole and undid the lock from inside, Clare smiled and muttered, "Call that subtle?"

When a neighbour appeared in the next garden, Clare called, "Police officers." She held up her warrant card for a moment before following Brett inside.

The house smelled musty, like a property that had not been used for a few days. Quickly, Brett and Clare checked the downstairs rooms to make sure that they were empty and then concentrated their efforts on the small, tidy living room. The decor was modern but inexpensive: a gas fire, a set of bookshelves containing big, dusty hardbacks from second-hand shops and a library's cast-off stock, a chest of drawers with a cheap midi hi-fi system on top, a telephone table, a television, a video and a small shelf containing video tapes. Clare pointed to the spine of one video box and remarked, "She's written *Pollution debate* on the side. I bet we know which programme that is."

"No pad by the telephone," Brett observed. He was hoping for a notebook that matched the kidnapper's.

Clare took a photograph of a woman from the top book shelf and examined it. Holding it by its brown cardboard frame, she ventured, "Not that different from the sketch."

Brett nodded. "We'll take it."

But they found nothing on Sheffield Cycling Club. The drawers and a cupboard were devoid of incriminating evidence. Nothing helpful at all.

"Let's spread out," Brett suggested. "I'll take upstairs while you finish off downstairs."

Brett discovered what he wanted in the first room that he tried: the spare bedroom. A big box file inscribed "SCC" was lying on the bed. He shouted for Clare and together they went through the papers inside. The alphabetical list of members did not include Alan Fox's name but Edward O Tarrant appeared towards the end. When they found the club's ROBS, Brett examined the frame numbers eagerly. The last entry confirmed it. The missing cycle was a blue mountain bike and its frame number was 01203775. Before it had been stolen, it had belonged to Edward O Tarrant.

"And then there were two," Brett murmured. He stared at the ceiling and wondered, "Sophie Dyer or Edward Tarrant. Which one of them wrote down the EOT message?"

Calmly, Clare replied, "I'd say it was Sophie Dyer."

Brett gazed first at his partner and then at the scrap of paper that she was holding out. It was a crumpled copy of a receipt for a membership fee. No doubt, Sophie had sent the original to the member but she had kept the duplicate. Across it was a carbon copy of the words that she had written on the original.

Paid by cheque. Recieved with thanks.

The writing and spelling looked familiar. Brett was nodding with a satisfied look on his face. "So, neither the kidnapper nor Sophie can spell received!" Leaving out three of the club's papers, Brett closed the file. "Let's go. We'll take the receipt, the lists of members and ROBS, and the photo."

Before they left, they peeked inside the other

bedroom. What they saw made them both stop and draw breath. In her bedroom, Sophie had indulged her infatuation with Phil. The walls were plastered with enlarged photographs of him. Shots of Phil outside his house, in his car, playing with Kerry in the wood, walking into work, walking away from work. Even outside the squash courts. He was pictured from every conceivable angle in rain, sunshine and snow. Smiling, sombre, tight-lipped, grinning, grimacing – every expression – but never looking into the camera lens. Only the bedroom door, light switch, window and ceiling were free of photographs. The rest of the room was devoted to Phil. The wallpaper had long since been submerged beneath overlapping snapshots. The private gallery had been arranged lovingly, scrupulously, compulsively. It must have taken hours. Some of the pictures were bent round the corners of the room, making it seem smaller, like a claustrophobic cave. Brett and Clare could imagine Sophie sitting in the room, gazing at the myriad pictures of Phil, surrounded by him, a warped smile on her face. There was no doubt that Sophie was infatuated. She had converted her bedroom into a shrine.

Brett exhaled and murmured, "Reminds me of that old song: *Every breath you take, every move you make, I'll be watching you.* Chilling."

"Let's get out of here," Clare whispered. "This gives me the creeps."

"Agreed. At least the first step's confirmed –

Sophie Dyer's the stalker."

"And how," Clare muttered.

On the way out, Brett said to his officers at the front of the house, "You're still on duty, I'm afraid. It looks like Sophie Dyer's the one we want. So no dropping off, right? You're on the front line, even if it doesn't feel like it. And," he jerked his thumb towards her front door, "call in a glazier, will you?"

While Clare drove back along busy roads towards the police station, Brett answered a call on his mobile phone. Phil Chapman's confident voice had been reduced to a quaking tremor. "We've just got another letter, Brett," he stammered.

Brett said into his phone, "Kerry's writing again?"

"Yes. Just like last time. It was posted yesterday in Sheffield."

"Locally," Brett murmured to himself. "OK, Phil," he said to his friend, "we *all* need to know what's in it. So open it now but use clean gloves and don't handle it more than you have to. Use tweezers if you like. You saw how I did the last one. Make sure you don't transfer anything to it or lose anything from it. I'm on my way to you, via headquarters. I'll get forensics to send someone over to collect it for tests. As soon as I've sorted that out and dropped something else off, I'll be straight over. Now, open it and tell me what it says."

"I'll do it now," Phil muttered.

There was a clatter as his nervous friend put down the phone.

In the traffic jam, Brett and Clare had travelled barely three hundred metres before Phil's voice sounded again. "It's strange," he said. "Nothing to do with H-Cars. I don't know what it means." Then he read out the message.

Soon you will join your real family. It is time to give up the woman who calls herself your wife and join the ones who really love you.

"I know what it means," Brett told Phil. "That something you had to give up wasn't a bit of chemistry. It's Chloe. That's what your stalker wants. Her name's Sophie Dyer and we can be pretty sure now she's got Kerry. It won't take me long to confirm it."

Brett decided not to upset Phil by describing the eccentric shrine. He turned off the phone and said, "OK, Clare, lights on. Barge your way through."

Handing over the copy of the receipt to Louise, Brett said, "Get it to George the graphologist. He'll know what I want. Is it the same writing as the first kidnap note? Tell him to call with the result."

"Before you go, Brett..." Louise waved towards the table where she had laid out all of the stills that she had requested from Phil's TV debate.

Brett scanned the photographs. Some showed close-ups of single spectators. Others were pictures of small groups of onlookers. There were wide-angle shots of the entire audience. One of the close-ups showed Naoki Matsumoto. Ross Mundee appeared in another, lurking behind a woman in the foreground. Brett also recognized Edward Tarrant at the front of the audience. After a couple of minutes, he spotted the person he was looking for. She *had* attended the debate herself. She looked just like the photograph in her living room. Sophie Dyer was sitting four rows back, avidly watching the proceedings, avidly watching Phil. In her frozen eyes, Brett could envisage the beginnings of an obsession. He got the impression that a bomb could have gone off in the vicinity of the TV studio and it would not have caused a ripple in her fixation.

Once Brett had finished examining the photographs, Louise recited the registration number of Dyer's Escort. "Good," Brett said. "Fast work." He assigned two of his team to house-to-house inquiries in Sophie Dyer's neighbourhood. "Build up a picture of her," he ordered. "Comings and goings, family, everything you can get." Then he dashed away with Clare.

Phil needed only a glance at the photograph of Sophie Dyer. "Yes, that's her," he declared.

Over his shoulder, Chloe agreed. "She's got Kerry, hasn't she?" Chloe cried. "I know it!"

"Yes," Brett replied. "Until the latest letter we were just guessing that she was playing at being Kerry's mother. Now it looks like we were right. Actually, it was Clare who got it right. Dyer regards herself as family, Kerry's mum. Sorry, Chloe."

"That's horrible!"

Brett put his hand on Chloe's shoulder. "Yes, but look at it like this. She won't hurt Kerry while she's using her as bait for Phil."

"Bait?"

Clare explained, "She's in a bad way. Seriously unbalanced. We believe that she thinks of herself as Phil's partner and Kerry as her daughter after an 'affair' of nine months. The new message confirms it. She's trying to unite her family. Luring Phil with Kerry."

"What do we do, then?" Phil enquired. "Go along with it till I can snatch Kerry back?"

"It might come to that. But it could take days," Clare answered. "You see, I think she's in no great hurry. She's waited for nine months. A few more days won't hurt her. She's probably taking her time for a reason. If I had to guess, I'd say she wants you to know what it's like to live without someone you love. Remember the first note? She wants you to feel what it's like to be incomplete. She's been that way for months. She's putting you through it, giving you a taste of her medicine, so you understand how she feels." Clare glanced at the gloomy face of her partner. She realized what was on his mind. Everyone in the room was enduring an enforced separation. Dragging her thoughts back to Phil and Chloe, Clare added a caution. "I have to say that going along with Sophie's plan isn't without danger."

"What danger?" Phil snapped.

Clare reasoned, "Once she's got you and Kerry with her, she may think of that moment as the highlight of her life. Somewhere inside her brain, she may just realize that it can't get any better. She might be tormented with the idea that you'll run out on her with Kerry. She'd do anything not to lose her instant family. She may think of a way to keep you for ever, to get out while she's on a high."

"What exactly are you saying?" Chloe gasped.

Clare had no option but to be honest and open with Brett's friends. "We're worried about suicide, Chloe. It's not unheard of. We're worried that, once she's got what she wants, she'll take out Phil and Kerry as well as herself."

Chloe fell back into her seat and stared at Clare in shock. "No!"

Aghast, Phil uttered, "Do you go along with all this mumbo-jumbo, Brett?" He wanted to hear it direct from his friend's mouth, scientist to scientist.

"Yes," Brett replied. "I'm afraid so." He glanced at his partner and then continued, "I'm convinced Clare's spot on. That's why we don't want to wait. I want to go after Dyer and catch her, before she gets too far with any plan she might have. I want Kerry back now."

"Where is she, then?" Phil asked.

Brett looked at the carpet as he responded, "That's the problem."

"You haven't got a clue, have you?" Phil muttered. He wasn't angry, just depressed.

Brett gazed at his friend. "Yes, I've got clues, Phil, plenty. But no strong lead. That's what I'm going back to work on now."

Phil squatted down to comfort his wife. "We know you're doing your best, Brett. Don't let us down."

16

Between mouthfuls of a huge baguette, Clare said, "Normally, I approve of women making inroads into male preserves, but not here. We should leave heavy crime to men. We women have got better sense – except Sophie Dyer. She's blinded by her passion." Clare swallowed hastily and added, "At least we know she's fairly local. She probably drove to her hideout on Monday night, sorted it out, and drove back to the Princess Street workshop first thing on Tuesday morning. And she was back in the Sheffield postal district yesterday to mail that letter."

"What else have we got?" Brett mused. He hoped for inspiration from those in the room but really he was talking to himself. The loose ends had already been tied up. Ed Tarrant verified that he'd telephoned the secretary of Sheffield Cycling Club last week and reported his bike missing. And, yes, its frame number was 01203775. His fingerprints did not match the ones on the dart flight found in the ruined workshop. George had declared himself to be 99.9 per cent sure that the words on the cycling-club receipt had been scribbled by the same person who had written the first kidnap note.

Brett was now convinced that he could prove that Sophie Dyer, the stalker and the kidnapper were all the same person. His theory explained why she had stopped stalking Phil. She was pursuing a different strategy to attach herself to him. She was using Kerry. The full search of her house had turned up very little to help locate Kerry but one significant find would help to convict Sophie Dyer. In her dustbin, there was a bedraggled and torn polyester coat in grey. There were no traces of Kerry in the house, so Brett deduced that Sophie had not taken Kerry home. She had probably gone directly to the arch workshop and from there to her present location. The latest letter in Kerry's handwriting had added nothing significant to Brett's chaotic list of evidence. Sophie was denying Brett vital evidence by getting her counterfeit daughter to write the letters.

The best facts, Brett told himself, were those that could link Sophie Dyer and Kerry with certainty. The deluge of data from Princess Street could have come from anywhere. Information from Sophie's house, like the Sheffield Cycling Club material and the coat, must have come from Sophie. If only there had been more of it. Evidence from the second letter might have indicated their whereabouts. But it had revealed nothing but the use of a disinfectant. Abruptly, Brett jumped up and commanded, "I want the search of Dyer's house, especially her rubbish, to be stepped up. Sift for receipts, invoices, anything bought on plastic. Where did she get that disinfectant from and what else did she buy at the same time? When she went shopping, she'd probably get everything she needed for this jaunt with Kerry, not just disinfectant. What else she bought might just tell us what she was planning. And what she was planning might just tell us where she is." He turned to his new assistant and said, "Get on the phone, Louise. That blue formalin solution—"

For the first time, Louise interrupted with confidence. "Yes. I'm on to it – who sells it?" Finally, her conviction matched her enthusiasm.

"Right," Brett pronounced. "I'm off to the library."

As soon as the door closed behind him, Louise looked over her monitor at Clare and whispered, "Library? I've never heard of a boss going to a library before."

"You haven't worked with Brett before," Clare replied. "He hasn't gone to get the new Dick Francis and put his feet up. Believe me, he'll come back with something." She brushed the crumbs from her lap and stood up, ready to join the ongoing search of Sophie Dyer's house. She had decided to take personal control.

By two-thirty in the afternoon, Louise, Clare and Brett had all come to the same conclusion: Sophie Dyer had absconded in a mobile home.

Louise had sounded out every likely shop and pharmacy in the local directory. Only three stocked the formalin solution. They were all camping and caravanning centres and the hazardous concoction was sold for disinfecting chemical toilets, the types used in caravans and on some camp sites. By questioning beyond her brief, Louise had established that on Monday evening Sophie Dyer had hired a small caravan from the Cosy Camping Centre. It was not the first time. She hired the same type of caravan on behalf of Sheffield Cycling Club every few months. The manager of the centre understood that Ms Dyer used it to ferry bikes to and from race meetings. The caravan served as a mobile base for the cycling team for the duration of the meet.

Clare had rescued a soggy, discoloured receipt from the dustbin that Sophie Dyer kept in her back yard. Not all of it could be read but it showed that Sophie had not just bought the disinfectant but also paid a deposit for the loan of something illegible. The bill included the projected cost of Calor gas, a fuel used mostly for heating, lighting and cooking in caravans.

In the reference library, Brett discovered that formalin was available to the public chiefly for killing germs in non-flushing toilets. Immediately, he thought of camping or caravanning. Formalin's toxic properties also made it ideal for embalming dead bodies, but Brett did not want to think about that possibility. He noted that the formaldehyde in the solution was an irritant and was cancer-forming. It could glue separate molecules together, making bigger, stronger ones, and was just as good at hardening plastics as gumming up the chemical interior of germs.

Much to Louise's surprise, when Brett returned from the library, he slammed his finger down on the ordnance survey map between Conisbrough and Doncaster. "That's my guess," he announced. "Somewhere along the A630."

Puzzled, Clare looked at her partner. "How come? What have you found?"

"Well, it's a bit of speculation but it's worth thinking about. In the arch workshop, there was mud from someone's shoe. It had particles of dolomite in it. Dolomite," he continued, "is a form of limestone: calcium magnesium carbonate, a creamy–yellow rock used for building stone and particularly in steel-making. So, it's mined near places with a steel industry, or places that used to have a decent steel industry. Plenty of mines near Sunderland to support Teeside steel works but Sophie's somewhere local. See these quarries along the A630? Particularly the two large ones? Guess what they produce."

Together, Clare and Louise chimed, "Dolomite."

Brett nodded. "Wonderful things, libraries.

Formalin, dolomite, steel industry. All the information's there." He put up his hands and said, "I know the objections. Any one of five hundred people could have left that mud behind. It's not a good lead because we can't say it definitely came from Dyer. Anyone could have picked up a bit of dolomite on a shoe near the quarries, in a storage facility, in a steel plant. But I called Roland Barnes and he told me the cycling club sometimes holds road races in the lanes around that area: Sheffield against Doncaster, South Yorkshire against Humberside. So, Sophie Dyer will know the place. It's still a long shot. If you've got any better ideas, let's get working on them."

Both Clare and Louise shook their head.

"Right. We run with it, then."

"There aren't any camp sites out that way, according to the map," Clare observed.

"The quarries aren't a pretty sight for tourists. But is that good or bad news? If I'm right, it'll be easier to spot a caravan on its own somewhere. It'll be good and conspicuous. On the other hand, it might mean I've got it all wrong."

"How do we check it out? I'm not sure how many cars I'll be able to commandeer."

"Forget it," Brett said. "Too slow and awkward. This is a job for the helicopter. It'll be much easier from the air. Then, if we get a sighting, we'll move in by car."

"If Dyer's there, won't the chopper be a bit of a giveaway?"

190

"It'll have to follow the road, like they do on traffic duty. No criss-crossing the area. No low swoops. If they spot something, they'll have to tell us and move on straightaway. So, let's commandeer the chopper."

Brett's foot soldiers returned wearily from Sophie Dyer's district bearing very little news. The neighbours knew next to nothing about her. "Kept herself to herself, she did." "Strong legs, I bet. All that cycling." "A few times, I saw her car towing away a caravan. That's all I know about her." "Never seen her have a visitor. Very solitary. It's not right for a young woman." "Seems to spend a lot of time away from the house." "I've seen her in the queue at the chemist getting photos developed. That's about it." And that *was* about it. No new information but a consistent picture of Sophie Dyer had emerged.

While Brett was busy justifying the diversion of the force's helicopter and gaining John Macfarlane's approval, Louise looked up from her computer and said, "You know, I can't find any camp sites in the area either, but –"

"What?"

"I've got a report of an affray here," she said, pointing to the map, a few miles out of Conisbrough. "Some travellers made camp along the A630 last week and tangled with the local hard cases."

"You're saying there's an unofficial gathering of caravans?"

Louise nodded. "Unless they've moved on."

"OK," Brett replied. "That's the first thing to

check out. She could have tagged on to the travellers."
He paced up and down, cursing, "Come on, come on.
Where's that helicopter? And someone make sure
we've got a radio link. I want to be in contact at all
times with the pilot."

"Pooh reporting for duty. Can you read me?"

"Pooh?" Brett queried.

"Just our little joke. Police officer on high." The
reception was distorted, as if the pilot was shouting
over a din, but his words were distinct.

"Where are you?" asked Brett into the radiophone
which a technician had delivered.

"Conisbrough, picking up the A630."

"What can you see?"

"Conisbrough," came the ironic response. "The
castle, railway, river, big viaduct, the water tower, the
sewage works. A sight for sore eyes."

Knowing that he wouldn't have a spy in the sky
for long, Brett ignored the pilot's sense of humour
and got on with the job. He had only one shot at
aerial surveillance. "You're looking for a parked
caravan."

"Yeah," the pilot shouted in reply. "Know them
well. When I'm driving, I always get stuck behind
one being towed in a narrow lane. Should be
banned."

"We've had notice of caravans by the A630. Are
they still there? That sort of thing." Brett found
himself yelling into the microphone as if the pilot

would have trouble hearing him over the racket of the engine and the rotor blades thwacking the air.

"Coming up to Cadeby Quarry, on the north side of the road. Looks like a great big bowl of chicken soup from up here. Lorries, shacks, spoil heap, but no caravans." To make sure that he'd been heard and understood, the airborne officer added, "No. Nothing."

"Keep going," Brett replied.

There was a pause.

"Still reading me?"

"Yes."

"I've got something. There's a lay-by and field just outside Warmsworth, by the turning for the landfill site and Dolomite Quarry." Through the irksome crackling he supplied a grid reference. "Looks like a gypsy camp to me. Five caravans as far as I can see."

Brett acknowledged the message. "Understood. Thanks. Press on towards Doncaster. Keep looking for a lone caravan." Brett was thinking about Kara's comment in Beaches. Sophie was not comfortable with strangers. He believed that she would shun them and find her own private spot.

The radio burst into life again. The voice of the helicopter pilot was still superimposed over the constant thrashing of blades. He reported, "That was the last working quarry before Doncaster. Still nothing."

"OK," Brett replied.

"You're definitely out of luck. No more caravans."

"Sure?"

"Yeah. Nothing. Look, I'm getting a message to divert north up the A1(M) to check out an obstruction. OK?"

Brett sighed. "I suppose so."

"Right, I'm wheeling north. Sorry I couldn't be of more help. Hope you get your caravan. All the best. Pooh over and out. That's just another little... Hang on. You might want to check this out. I just got a flash of something – a roof? – on my left. In Scabba Wood. Just north of a small quarry. It's another landfill site now, west of Sprotbrough." Again, he gave a map reference. "There's not supposed to be anything in there but trees, so you'd do well to give it the once-over. I saw *something*."

"Stationary?"

"I think so."

"Can you confirm what it was?" Brett asked.

"Not a hope. Not without circling. It was a split-second glimpse in the distance. Want me to circle?"

"No," Brett said. "Any chance it was a caravan, though?"

"Yeah. Or a car, or a van, or a hut. Or an alien spacecraft."

"All right. I get the picture. We'll take it from there. Thanks. Go and sort out the motorway."

"Good luck. Pooh over and out."

Brett shut down the radio, dropped it on to the table and said to Clare, "Come on. No point hanging around. Let's go. Just the two of us first." To Louise, he said, "Stay here. If we need troops, I'll call. In the meantime, make sure the whole team's available. Drop all other lines of inquiry. Bring them in and keep them here on stand-by."

The travellers were not doing any harm but, wherever they put down temporary roots, they were hounded by the locals and the authorities. As a result, they had learnt to recognize trouble at fifty paces, either vigilante thugs or police officers. Years of aggravation had taught them to be defensive and uncooperative. Now, distrust was ingrained in them.

Brett did not have to show his ID to the two travellers who walked assertively towards him. "Cops," they grunted. "What do you want? Have you caught the lads who attacked us?"

"It's something else," Brett replied. "You might be able to help me." He held out photographs of Sophie and Kerry and asked, "Have you seen this woman, with the girl?"

"Why should we?"

On the makeshift site, which spilled across the lay-by and into the adjoining field, all of the caravans were large and had seen many years of use. None of them had an Escort parked alongside. Most had been towed by vans. "I can see she's not with you," Brett said, "but I want to know if she's been around, perhaps wanting to join up with you."

"What's she done?" the one with the beard asked suspiciously.

"The girl doesn't belong to her," Brett answered, trying to be patient. "Her mum and dad want her back. I'm sure you can imagine. Just think if it was one of your girls who'd been taken. Now, have you seen her?" He thrust the photos forward.

Both of the men squinted at the prints. The sunlight reflected off the glossy surfaces, blotting out the images, but neither of them persevered or shifted to a different angle. "We'll let you know if we do."

From one of the caravans, a clothes line ran from the roof to the ground. Every time a car or lorry pounded along the busy A630, the garments were buffeted and flapped about like pennants on a guy rope. Between the roar of passing traffic, there was the distant clatter of mined stone being forced along conveyor belts and falling into containers at the quarry. Littered around another of the caravans, there was a collection of lawnmowers and trimmers of all shapes and sizes. Obviously, one of the travellers was earning some cash by taking on some gardening jobs. Outside another, an elderly lady sat in an incongruous armchair, knitting children's clothes.

"How about this?" Clare chipped in. "A hired caravan pulled by a white Escort. Have you seen one round here?"

The men glanced at each other before one replied, "Yeah. Cars, lorries, caravans, camper vans, helicopters, motorbikes. You name it, we've seen it."

On cue, an empty dustcart and a huge lorry carrying dolomite emerged from the side road, marked by creamy-coloured boulders. The trucks rumbled past and pale dust was shaken from the load of rocks, cascading on to the road and verge. The ground, impregnated with small yellow chips of stone, quaked beneath Brett's feet.

The other traveller muttered, "Picturesque here, isn't it?"

"So, you haven't seen a white Escort coming and going a lot?"

"The kid's wanting to go home, is she?"

Brett nodded. "I know her. Yes, believe me, she wants to go home. She's being held against her will."

The traveller stared into Brett's eyes as if assessing his honesty. After a few seconds, he said, "Try the wood up the road. Left at the lights and left again. You never know." Together, the two men turned and sauntered away. They would say no more.

Off the main road, Clare and Brett found themselves on a quiet residential avenue that ran over the railway line, and then became a claustrophobic, steep and twisty lane down to and over the River Don. The narrow road brushed against Scabba Wood. Clare did not stop. First she wanted to reconnoitre the area. She drove past the track that led into the wood and cruised up the lane until she left behind the last line of trees. Then she turned the car around using the deserted entrance to Scabba Wood Quarry Landfill site and crawled back again. The wood was dense with beeches, yew and sycamore, and it was bordered with barbed wire. It would be difficult for a person on foot to enter it. Certainly, a car and caravan could have only gone in via the track. She parked on the crooked verge, not encroaching on the trail that led into the wood. With Brett, she got out, stretched, and surveyed the area. An iron gate, chained to a sturdy post, blocked off the dirt track. Attached to one of the bars was a sign: *Trespassers will be prosecuted*. The forestry site was out of bounds.

Brett shrugged and led the way to the gate. He grabbed the padlock and found that it was broken. "Not as inaccessible as it looks," he commented, swinging the gate open. The dirt track was wide enough for a vehicle and, according to the map, it came to a dead end in a field on the other side of the wood. Immediately Brett noticed that small pieces of dolomite were embedded in the track. On either side of the trail, the woodland would be difficult to penetrate. There were no paths and the undergrowth was thick with brambles, giant bellflower and nettles.

The trees were disordered obstacles. In the late afternoon air, there was the distant drone of tractors and diggers shunting rubbish around the landfill site but, much closer, there was loud birdsong. Wren, blackcap and willow warbler contributed to the cheerful chorus.

"Good hiding place," Clare observed. "Everyone's frightened off by the sign. And no one can see into it, except from the air."

"If Sophie Dyer's got a hired caravan in here, it'll have to be near the track. There's nowhere else to get a car and caravan. Besides, from the helicopter, it'd just be a mass of branches and leaves, except for this path."

"So, are we going in?" Clare asked. "Are we going to risk prosecution for trespass?"

"Sure are. I'll just let Louise know."

Using the car radio, Brett updated his assistant and then rejoined Clare. Together they probed deeper into Scabba Wood. They did not want to alert Sophie, if she was secreted inside, to their arrival by driving along the track. Instead, they explored the trail on foot.

"If we come across her car and caravan," Brett warned Clare, "we're going to have to pretend to be enjoying a quiet romantic stroll, in case she sees us."

"Just like the case started," Clare remarked. She nudged him and said impishly, "I've never worked so closely with anyone before."

Brett's smile was more troubled than wholehearted.

As they walked further and further into the wood, scattering butterflies from the edges of the path, they were reduced to whispers and frequently to silence. Either side of them, brown pillars held up a thick canopy that did not quite meet above their heads. The rich foliage kept most of the strong sunlight at bay. There was much more shade than there were shafts of light among the trees. The path itself, though, was a bright stripe carved through the middle of the wood. Brett and Clare concentrated on the gently curving path in front of them. They were hoping to see a caravan and white Escort, but they knew that they were more likely to stumble across a cabin or a truck for forestry workers.

Overhead, the birds still fluttered and called out in tuneful language. To Clare's left, there was a sudden scrabbling noise as a startled woodmouse made a dash for safety.

Abruptly and powerfully, Clare grabbed Brett's arm and yanked him to the right-hand side of the path. They halted.

"Yes," Brett whispered. "I see it."

Ahead of them, a white caravan had been manoeuvred into a small turning place. From where they were, they could just make out its front corner. Beyond that, they noticed the bonnet of a white Escort jutting out on to the driveway.

"It's going to be tricky to get to it through the trees," Brett judged. "They'd give us great cover but it's too thick. We'd stumble all over the place in the undergrowth."

"We may have to," Clare said under her breath. "But right now, we're out of sight of the windows. Let's get closer along the track."

Brett nodded and together they crept forward, a step at a time. Luckily, the tree-lined lane was laid with compacted earth. The detectives' footfalls were almost noiseless. The bits of dolomite were not loose but embedded into the surface so Brett and Clare could walk without crunching stone.

With the caravan still some distance away, the first window came into view. Brett breathed a sigh of relief. "The curtain's drawn," he murmured. "We can get closer." He squatted, out of sight, just in case someone looked out.

Clare also crouched down. "We'll have to be careful," she advised. "The curtain's drawn but the window's open a bit."

"I guess it'd be stifling in there without a window open."

"Yeah," Clare agreed in a whisper. "But it means we'll be very easy to hear if we go much closer. We won't be able to make a sound without telling everyone we're here."

Brett sighed. "I know."

Clare muttered, "Wouldn't you just love to know what's going on in there?"

Brett glanced at her. "More than that. I'd love to crash in right now and have done with it."

"But you won't," Clare replied anxiously. "Too dangerous. We might be very close to rescuing Kerry. You can't risk macho rush-and-push tactics now."

"I know. Softly, softly. That's what it says in the manual for hostage situations."

"We need surveillance here, Brett. We need all their fancy listening gear to tell us who's inside and what they're saying."

"More than that," Brett replied. "I'd like to *see* inside as well." He stood up but moved to the right to keep the trunk of a beech between himself and the window. "You stay here and keep watch, Clare. I'm going to recruit a new member of the team."

"What?" Clare hissed.

"You'll see," Brett replied. He held out his hand for the car key.

"And what if the caravan moves out? Do you expect me to jump on it as it goes past, James Bond-style?"

"As soon as I get back to the car, I'll sort it out. There's only three roads out of here. I'll get un-marked cars stationed on each one, just in case. You'll have back-up while I'm gone. I'll see you here in, I don't know, about an hour and a half, OK?"

Clare nodded.

While he drove back to Sheffield at speed, Brett called the university. He aimed to give Professor Matsumoto as much advance notice as possible. That way, Naoki could get everything ready and, when Brett arrived, they could leave for Scabba Wood straightaway. When Brett got through to the technologist, he asked bluntly, "Can you control your Robotroach remotely with a portable computer?"

"Of course. That's how we'd need to manipulate him in most circumstances, such as an earthquake. Why do you ask?"

"Because I want to offer you something. A unique opportunity to test your device. A proper field trial, as you called it yesterday."

Eagerly, the professor asked, "What? A landslide, collapsed building?"

"A hostage in a caravan. I want to know what's going on before I risk storming in there."

"When?"

"I'm closing in on you now. I'm about five miles away."

"I was just about to leave work, but not now," Naoki replied. "I'll help, with one condition."

"What's that?" Brett snapped, not expecting to have to barter over saving Kerry's life.

"You let me write up the results like a scientific experiment and show it to my sponsors. They'll be very impressed if Robbie solves a problem for the police force. Very impressed means very generous with funding."

"It's a deal," Brett agreed.

"I'll get ready," Naoki chirped. "See you soon."

By phone, Brett informed Phil and Chloe of developments but did not invite them to join the operation. He needed to be surrounded by clear-headed professionals, not by fraught parents. He did not request marksmen. He would not expose a seven-year-old to a gun battle and endanger her life with stray bullets. Instead, he procured a small posse of cars to position at strategic points around the lanes that encompassed Scabba Wood. The triangle made by Cadeby, Sprotbrough and High Melton would be quietly seething with anonymous officers. If Sophie was holed up there, Brett was determined to prevent her slipping away with Kerry. When he returned to the wood, he had Louise, Naoki and Robotroach with him, and several unmarked cars following behind. He had brought Louise as part of her training and so that she could act as liaison by mobile phone. By the time that Brett approached Sprotbrough, she had relayed his orders to each officer in the convoy of cars. Brett had also briefed both Louise and Naoki on the siege situation and the need for quiet. He parked his own car across the track, blocking the caravan in the wood. The rest of his team spread out around the forestry site like a police cordon. If Sophie was in the caravan, she was totally hemmed in.

It was six forty-five when the three of them walked cautiously down the track towards Clare and the caravan. The sun was lower in the sky and the shadows were longer and more angled. Naoki was carrying a laptop computer, transmitter and a small box containing Robotroach.

Clare had merged herself so completely with the undergrowth at the right of the track – still in view of the caravan window – that she had to draw Brett's attention to her. "Psst!" she called quietly. She had cleared a small area where they could all keep watch, squatting down or sitting on a tree stump. Clare left the flat stump as a seat for Professor Matsumoto. With the portable computer balanced on his lap, he adjusted the glasses on his nose and began to prepare Robotroach.

"Ah," Clare murmured. "So that's your new recruit. Not you, Louise. Something altogether smaller."

"Any developments?" Brett enquired.

"No. But there *is* someone in there, I'm sure. I think I heard a thud from inside. Maybe something falling and hitting the floor."

"Robbie's ready for action," Naoki announced in a whisper.

Brett asked, "If we let it go from here, it'll take an age to crawl to the caravan, won't it?"

"Absolutely. A very long time," Naoki agreed. "It'd be best to release him on to a surface inside the caravan. If not, then the outside surface by an open window. Then I can guide him in."

Pointing through the trees, Brett said, "How about that? See? The open window."

Naoki nodded. "That'll do. But it wouldn't be a good idea to put him on the curtain. A gust of wind or another sudden movement of the curtain and he'd be off. A solid surface, flat or vertical, it doesn't matter, would be better."

Both Brett and Clare sucked in air. "Tricky," Brett breathed. "With the window open, anyone inside will hear the slightest noise. If we're going to take Robotroach to the window, we'll have to do it in total silence."

"It's either that or a long wait," the professor said plainly.

"I'll take it," Clare volunteered. "I'm lightest on my feet. I'm most likely to be able to do it without making any noise."

"Sure?" Brett asked.

In answer, Clare held out her flattened hand towards Naoki. Insects weren't her favourite creatures but she wasn't squeamish about touching them. The one that Naoki placed carefully on her palm made her shiver not because it was a cockroach but because it had been mutilated. It was a distasteful hybrid of insect and machine. It was also worth half a million pounds – the most valuable thing she had ever held in her hand. But it could help them save Kerry.

"Grip him lightly by his backpack," Naoki advised her. "Between thumb and forefinger. He won't struggle or try to go anywhere until I give him the signal." He patted his portable computer.

Brett murmured to his partner, "Good luck. Take care."

To try and steady her nerves, Clare joked, "Gives a whole new meaning to planting a bug, doesn't it?"

With the delicately modified Robotroach gripped between her fingers, she stood, took a deep breath and began her surreptitious approach. At first, she crept along the edge of the track but soon realized that she was too visible. She made her way into the wood itself, hoping to slip stealthily from tree to tree for protection. It wasn't easy. Without a path, she had to pick a meandering route, avoiding the worst of the tangled undergrowth, while making sure that she didn't drop her weird cargo, make a sound, or reveal herself.

A few metres away from the caravan, she hesitated behind a tree. She thought that she'd heard a voice, possibly adult, certainly female. Clare rested her free hand on the trunk of the tree while she strained to listen. If there had been a voice, it had subsided. She peeked at the caravan. The side facing her contained the door and a single window. There was no sign of activity.

Clare watched as an ugly devil's coach horse crawled from the bark and on to the back of her hand. She let it explore her skin because she didn't want to make any sudden movements or noise. Rather, she adopted a wry grin. With a cockroach grasped in her right hand, a black beetle strolling over her left, it was lucky that she didn't have a phobia about insects.

When she moved again, she blew the beetle from her hand then took a step, but her trailing leg was ensnared by a bramble and she nearly toppled on to the ground with a thump. Using her practised sense of balance, she hopped back and managed to remain upright, then froze behind the sycamore. In stumbling, she had rustled the undergrowth loudly. She tried to breathe normally as she sensed the curtain in the caravan twitching and saw Sophie's wild face appearing briefly at the window. Clare was not anxious for herself. If she made a mistake, she would not suffer for it. She was on edge because it was a small girl who would pay for any failing by her. It was Kerry who was in peril.

Clare waited for two minutes before she dared to attempt the final approach again. She shook the bramble off her leg and in retaliation the barbed plant ripped into her flesh through her thin trousers. Clare bit her lip to stop herself issuing a pained, "Ouch!"

After three tortuously slow steps through the snarled undergrowth, Clare had to negotiate a small stream in a muddy trench. Under normal circumstances, she would have leapt over it easily and landed with hardly a sound on the other side but having Robotroach in one hand and being in full view of the window, she didn't want to risk it. She padded gingerly down the slope, through the trickle of muddy water, and up on to a slab of dolomite. Emerging from the last line of trees, she was within a couple of paces of the caravan. If, on a whim, Sophie decided to look out again or come to the door, Clare would be right in front of her.

Clare ducked down. This way, there was a chance that an inquisitive Sophie at the window might simply peer over her head and not see the stooping police officer. She crawled up to the caravan and sat down beside it.

There was a clunk as something inside hit the wall of the caravan. It was as if someone had thrown a small object against the side. "Look," a chastizing voice sounded from within, "I'm doing my best to get you back together with your dad. Now behave or you'll *never* see him again. Take it and write exactly what I say. Remember last time you played up? You know what happened, don't you? I had to shut you in that horrid workshop to calm you down. If you'd come willingly, if you'd been good, I wouldn't have had to do that. I don't think you want me to do it again, do you? I think you'd prefer to have your dad. So, start to write."

Clare hoped that, while Sophie was lecturing Kerry, she would not be paying much attention to events outside. Still keeping low, Clare reached up with her right hand and placed Robotroach against the side of the caravan just below the open window. She was loath to let go of the insect because she had the awful feeling that it might not cling to the surface. It might fall on to her or on to the ground and be lost, or its electronic box of tricks damaged. Slowly, she unclenched her fingers, ready to grip again if Robotroach showed any sign of slithering down the side – but it didn't. Steadfastly, it clung to the vertical exterior. Clare sat there for a while and kept her eye on Robotroach to make sure that it was stable. After a moment, it moved a little to the right then jerkily upward, closer to the window. Clare smiled with relief. She guessed that Naoki was in control, trying to tell her that all was well with his invention. On hands and knees she scrambled quietly away. This time, she jumped sleekly over the stream. She landed silently on the other side and took refuge for a few seconds behind another tree. Peering out from behind the trunk, she checked that there was no further commotion back at the caravan. It was still. All she saw was the back end of Robotroach disappearing on to the lip of the window under the gently stirring curtain.

Still treading deliberately and choosing a route for maximum cover, Clare made her way cautiously back to her colleagues.

Brett nodded towards her as she crouched down in the rough den. "Well done," he said. "Look, you've cracked it."

The three of them were huddled round the computer like youngsters plotting mischief. Clare joined them. On the screen of the portable computer was displayed an insect-eye view of the caravan. Naoki was commanding Robbie to crawl along the narrow window ledge and slowly rotate to scan the entire mobile home. At the same time, his microphone picked up any sounds. First, the camera was pointing to the right, showing the top of the Calor gas cooker and, beyond it, bunk beds. The picture was in black and white, clear but distorted. It was difficult to gauge distances. The foreground seemed too close and more distant objects looked artificially small, too far away. As Naoki hit the space bar, Robotroach began to swivel. The unmade bunk beds disappeared and an internal door came into view. "That'll be opposite the main door," Naoki said. "A wardrobe?"

"Too large," Brett ventured. "More likely a shower and toilet compartment."

Still turning to the left, the camera panned across

a storage unit and then focused on a long seat that extended into the far corner of the caravan. They all breathed in as Sophie Dyer was revealed. She was seated, leaning on the table in front of her and concentrating intently.

"Keep going," Brett urged. "There'll be another bench on the other side of the table. It's one of those units where the table top drops down into the gap between the seats and takes a mattress to form a double bed."

"The angle's severe," Naoki said apologetically as he continued to turn his pet device. "The picture will be very distorted."

But it wasn't so deformed that Brett could not recognize his godchild at the extreme left of the monitor. She was sitting opposite Sophie, writing on a pad. Her face, disfigured by the miniature camera, clearly showed tears. She was wearing new clothes that did not suit her at all. The computer's speakers emitted the pitiable sound of her sobbing and sniffing. Brett could not understand how anyone could fail to be moved by her obvious distress. But Sophie was oblivious to it. "That's it," she was saying. "Just sign it and it's done."

The fountain pen fell from Kerry's right hand and her head dropped on to the table. "Will Dad come now?" she mumbled through her weeping.

"Yes, of course he will," Sophie said excitedly. "Not straightaway, but he will. He'll join us. You see, you've written the instructions yourself. I wouldn't lie to you. Now, do the envelope and stick the stamp on."

Brett swore under his breath and then pointed to the screen. "Look. Only her right hand's free. The left's shackled to something. I can't make it out."

Clare peered at the monitor and commented, "Looks like a bike chain and padlock."

Brett and Louise shook their heads sadly. Only Naoki seemed pleased. And he was only pleased because Robotroach was working perfectly. He wasn't enjoying the painful pictures.

"What are we going to do?" Clare prompted.

"Wait for a few minutes," Brett whispered. He wasn't being indecisive. There was the possibility of rescuing Kerry quickly and easily. It just needed a bit of patience.

Eventually, Sophie grabbed the letter in her gloved hands and pushed it into the addressed envelope. She held it out to Kerry and ordered, "Lick it. Come on! I can see you've got plenty of spit." After Kerry had moistened the envelope, Sophie took it back, sealed it and stood up, saying, "Right, I'm going to post it. Then it'll be away first thing in the morning."

It was exactly what Brett was hoping for. Immediately, he swung into action.

"That's it!" he exclaimed. "Our cue." Hurriedly, he gave the car key to Clare and said, "The car's blocking the track. You know what to do?"

"Sprint back and shift it. Hide it. Then come out and follow her."

Brett nodded. "Radio the other cars to close in and block her in the lane. Then we've cracked it. We've got them both, separated."

It could not have worked out better. The plan relied only on Clare beating Sophie back to the exit on to Cadeby Lane.

"Go, go," Brett urged.

Clare rose and slipped out of their hiding place. At first she kept to the edge of the track where she was less likely to be seen when Sophie emerged from the caravan. Then, when she was out of sight, she abandoned discretion and ran along the track as fast as she could.

Unseen, Robotroach had tracked Sophie across the caravan. She stood at the door and said to Kerry, "I won't be long. When I come back, I'll read you that story again – the princess, the handsome father and the unfaithful mother."

It was obvious that Kerry was not in the mood for a story but Sophie ignored the girl's misery. Clearly, the promised reading was for her benefit and not for Kerry's. The watchers in the wood could not see Kerry's response, but the sound was unmistakable. She was banging desperately on the table with her free arm, or with her head. Perhaps Sophie regarded Kerry's grief as a trivial, temporary and justifiable inconvenience. Perhaps she believed that everything would be all right once she had lured Kerry's dad into her lair. Perhaps she believed that her cruelty would be forgotten and forgiven on his arrival.

"All right," Brett whispered. "Turn the sound off, Naoki. Everyone duck down, and no talking. She mustn't see or hear us." He was within seconds of rescuing his goddaughter without even a confrontation. He could hardly believe his luck.

They heard the caravan door opening, Sophie stepping down on to the soil and keys jangling. They could picture her locking the door and then walking around the caravan towards the car, but they did not attempt to watch.

It was at that moment that Louise's mobile began to chirp loudly above the birdsong.

19

Sophie stopped dead. She paused for a second and then dashed back to the door. Hastily, she unlocked it, re-entered the caravan and slammed the door shut.

There was no time for blame and recriminations. No time to tell Louise that mobile phones should always be turned off during undercover operations. Instead, Brett almost pushed her out of the undergrowth. Urgently, he whispered, "Answer it! Walk down the track towards the caravan. You're enjoying a stroll. Stop in full view. Say into the phone, "All right, I'll come back now." Make it loud. Then ring off, turn round and walk away. Then go and tell Clare what's happened."

He was hoping that Louise could convince Sophie that there was nothing sinister in the sudden sound of a telephone. He was hoping that Sophie would not assume that she had been rumbled, that she was surrounded by police. There was a chance that he could avoid a difficult hostage situation if Louise undid her unfortunate blunder and gave a good performance as a young woman out for a casual stroll. Luckily, she did not look like a police officer. She did not have the right air of authority. The mobile phone and the hand that held it partly obscured a face that was as pink as Clare's nose after a day in the sun.

Louise stopped walking and said into the phone, "But I'm out getting some fresh air."

To Brett, her utterance did not sound natural. It was the quaking voice of an acutely embarrassed person. But he was relying on Sophie not identifying her odd manner as nerves.

After a few seconds, feigning annoyance, Louise said, "Oh, all right. I'll come back straightaway." She put the phone in her bag, shook her head exaggeratedly, spun round and marched away.

Keeping low, Brett glanced at Naoki and his computer screen, which was virtually black. Naoki had the volume on so softly that he had to put his ear against the computer to hear it. "Has she said anything?" Brett asked in a whisper.

"No," Naoki answered quietly. "But the girl asked why she went back in." He increased the volume slightly.

Suddenly anxious, Brett said, "If Sophie went to the window to check what Louise was doing, won't she have seen your Robbie?"

"Almost certainly," Naoki replied. "That's why I walked him to the floor as soon as the phone rang."

Brett nodded in appreciation of the professor's quick thinking. "Where is it now?"

"Under the bunk beds," he said, while he fiddled with the instruction program. "A bit dark for this version of the camera. I'm trying to get him poking out into the light and pointed down the length of the caravan. You'll see more legs than anything else but it's better than nothing."

In the renewed quiet, Brett could just hear Sophie's words. "I've decided not to go," she snapped at Kerry.

"Why?" Kerry cried in a broken voice. "I want my dad."

"So do I," Sophie replied. "But…" She sat down on the edge of the seat.

Robotroach's camera captured Sophie's whole frame, but the distance between her shoes and knees was greater than the length of the rest of her body. She looked as if she had been pictured in a joke fairground mirror. But it wasn't funny.

Talking to herself, she muttered, "No one comes here. It's private land. They go up the road to Melton Wood for walks. It's got nature trails."

Brett groaned. "She's on to us," he muttered.

Sophie drew back the curtain and opened the window fully. She shouted into the wood, "I know you're out there!"

Brett glanced at Naoki and put his forefinger to his lips. He hoped that silence might persuade her that she was wrong.

"Who is it?" she yelled.

Without a response to her shout, she withdrew from the window.

Brett studied the computer screen once more. Sophie was mumbling incomprehensibly to herself. She was digging inside her handbag madly, casting out unwanted items. They fell dramatically like parachutes in front of Robotroach's video camera. Finally, she found a small key, then headed over to Kerry.

"I don't think this is good news," Brett murmured fearfully.

Through the speakers, Kerry squealed, "What's going on? What are you doing? Are you letting me go?"

Sophie's body, bending over Kerry, hid what she was doing, but it sounded as if she was removing the padlock that secured Kerry's left hand to the bench. Then Sophie wrapped the chain around her own wrist to manacle Kerry to her and dragged the petrified girl to the door. The computer screen cut off Sophie's head but it showed her leaning into the toilet unit, grabbing a heavy plastic container and unscrewing its top with her left hand. Coming closer to the camera, Kerry's head was also sliced from the computer image. Instead, the screen was filled with Sophie's leg kicking the door open.

In the doorway, Sophie clasped Kerry firmly in front of her. In her left hand the stalker held the opened container of coloured formalin disinfectant. Slowly, she tilted it, threatening to pour it over Kerry's head. "Come out!" she screamed.

In horror, Brett saw her through the trees. He knew all about formalin. In bugs it acted by binding together the proteins that were essential for life, stopping them working. It killed germs at once. It did the same thing to the proteins in human eyes. A dose of just two grammes of formalin would obliterate the retina. Blindness was inevitable.

Brett did not have a choice. He stood up, walked on to the track and took a few paces until he was visible to Sophie and Kerry.

Kerry gasped and cried, "Brett!"

Her cry tore into Brett's heart. He was so close to her, but helpless.

Sophie glanced down at her hostage. "You know him?"

Kerry was almost speechless with fear and anticipation. She could only nod.

"Who are you?" Sophie demanded.

"Brett Lawless. Just a friend of the family."

Sophie eyed him distrustfully. "Not the police?"

Brett smiled. "With a name like Lawless? You've got to be joking. Besides, you told Phil not to involve the police." He wasn't sure if he could gain any advantage from the bluff but he wasn't yet ready to admit the reality of the situation. He thought that

Sophie might react aggressively if she knew that she was caught at the centre of a web woven by the police.

Frowning, she said, "I've seen you before. Are you the one who plays squash with him?"

"Yes, that's it," Brett replied, realizing that she must have noticed him at the squash club. Anyway, it seemed to reassure her, as if police officers were forbidden to play squash.

"How did you know I was here?"

Needing to contrive a story rapidly, Brett shrugged. "I didn't. But I reckoned you were in this general area."

"Why?" Sophie demanded to know, still holding the formalin aloft.

Making it up as he went along, Brett answered, "Well, you know Phil's a chemist. He analyzed one of your letters. Found dolomite dust on it." He kicked a rock lying at the edge of the track. "That's dolomite. This area is riddled with the stuff. So I was touring around, just in case I found you."

"Why isn't Phil here as well, then?"

"We split up to cover the ground quicker. He's searching nearer to Conisbrough."

"Who was the girl with the phone?"

"Louise," Brett answered. "A friend. She knows the area better than me so she was helping out. My tour guide."

"All right," Sophie said, apparently taken in by Brett's fairy tale. "If you don't want Kerry to be hurt, you'd better get Phil here, on his own. Get your friend Louise to call him."

"He'll come if you release Kerry," Brett called. "That's the best way. I'll take her back."

"No!" Sophie bellowed. "Kerry stays here. When Phil comes, we'll be complete at last. A family."

"I don't think—"

"Either he comes here or he never sees his daughter again. If I don't have him, he won't have his daughter, ever. And you can tell him that. I've booby-trapped the caravan. Phil will understand. If you try anything, it's goodbye to Kerry. Now, go and tell Phil. Send him here on his own."

"All right," Brett conceded. "I'll do it." To Kerry he shouted some words of encouragement. "It won't be long, Kerry. Hold on."

Brett walked purposefully away until he heard the caravan door close and the turning of the key in the lock. Sophie was making sure that no one could storm her refuge and take her by surprise. Brett stopped, turned and made his way furtively back to Naoki. Squatting next to the technologist, he asked, "Anything?"

"She's opened all the curtains so she can see anyone approaching, and she's chained Kerry to the table again. That's all. And she's been growling to herself. She's –" Naoki put a finger to the side of his head.

"Crazy?" Brett suggested.

"Yes," Naoki agreed. "Dangerous."

"Can you make Robotroach wander around? She says she's booby-trapped the caravan. Has she? Or is she bluffing? See if you can see anything through the camera. If she has, I've got to know what it is."

"I'll try," Naoki replied.

While the robotics maestro programmed his insect slave, Brett murmured to himself, "What did she mean when she said, 'Phil will understand'? Understand why she'd done it? Understand the booby-trap?" In frustration, Brett shook his head. He also wondered what Louise and Clare were doing and where they were. He knew that it was no use trying to call them. After the disaster that had turned a simple and swift operation into a waking nightmare, Louise would have turned off her phone.

Robotroach had climbed up the leg of the bunk and was surveying the caravan from the blanket on the bed. Luckily, the blanket was dark so the insect would not be easy for Sophie to spot. But the camera was not high enough to see on to the work surfaces and the table. Naoki instructed Robotroach to clamber up the wall to the top bunk, where the camera would be able to peer down on most of the caravan.

During the laborious climb, the insect transmitted only useless wobbly pictures of the ceiling. The microphone picked up Kerry's continual weeping and Sophie's impatient mumblings.

Eventually, under Naoki's expert control, Robotroach reached the top bunk and manoeuvred the camera into position. To the right, the shower and toilet unit did not appear suspect, but Sophie could have tampered with something inside. It would be another long trek for Robotroach to go back down to the floor and try to get into the compartment through a gap under its door. Then, if any of the disinfectant had been spilled inside, it would kill him. Brett had to remember that Robotroach was still a living creature and not a machine. Instead, Naoki programmed his captive cockroach to pan round the rest of the interior. Beyond the toilet, there were cupboards set in the apex of the wall and ceiling. They extended right over the seat occupied by Sophie, the window at the front of the caravan and Kerry's bench. They did not seem to be unusual in any way. No wires or dubious devices were showing.

Beside Kerry there was a draining board, a sink and a cooker. It was when the camera scanned the gas hob that Naoki's finger stopped tapping at the space bar. Along with Brett, he peered at the monitor.

"Yes," Brett murmured. "Something's not quite right there. The burners have been removed!"

Naoki pointed to the adjacent work surface. Next to the soap, there was a box of matches and a candle.

Brett gasped. "She's doctored the cooker to turn it into a furnace – or a bomb. If she got Phil in there, she'd fill the place with Calor gas and torch it. Clare was right. She wants to end it all with her new 'family' while she's got them together."

"Perhaps that's why she said Dr Chapman would

understand," Naoki said dolefully. "He knows all about the burning of different fuels."

Brett nodded slowly. "What's more," he muttered to himself, "she might blow up the caravan with just her and Kerry inside if she thinks she's not going to get Phil." He shuddered.

20

Brett looked up to the sky as if for inspiration. It was about half an hour from sunset. After that, the summer twilight would persist for another hour. At least he would not have to contend with complete darkness for a while.

"I'd say you've got a problem," Naoki whispered sympathetically. "You bring in Dr Chapman and you've got the possibility of progress, and the possibility that she'll kill all three. Keep him out of it and you lose the chance of progress, but her target's down to two. A moral dilemma."

Brett glanced at his amateur helper and replied, "Not really. You see, I've already made the decision to keep Phil away. I'd put him in too much danger if I brought him here. And I don't accept that there's only one alternative. There are always other options,

227

other ways of progressing. It's just a matter of spotting them. Right now, there's one obvious thing I need."

"Oh?"

"The source of the fuel – the Calor gas cylinder. We haven't seen it through Robotroach's camera. So where is it?"

"I see what you mean," Naoki replied. "Cut off the gas and she can't blow up the caravan. The main threat's gone." He turned his attention back to his computer. "I'll get him working on it. It'll take time."

"First, try the cupboard under the gas cooker, if he can crawl into it." Brett paused and then changed his mind. "Even better, move him to the back of the hob. There must be a pipe that delivers the gas. If you can get him on to the pipe, perhaps he can walk back along it till he gets to the cylinder."

Without looking up from the laptop, Naoki said, "Fine in theory but it'll probably be too dark to see anything. And if the woman decides to make a cup of tea…"

They both looked round as a breathless Louise joined them. She squatted down, hardly daring to look into Brett's face. "I'm sorry, Brett." She shook her head, still annoyed with herself. "Anyway," she reported, "I spoke to Clare. She said to tell you she's racing right round the wood so she can take up position on the other side. If you can distract Dyer from this side, she'll move in from the other if she gets the chance."

Brett nodded. "Good. Gives us another option. For now, though," he said, looking at Naoki, "I need to know where the Calor gas is. You're worried your Robotroach will be roasted. Let me ask you this: can you make another one?"

"Given time and money, yes, I'll make another, and another," Professor Matsumoto said. "I always intended to. With improvements. Your point is, that no amount of time and money can make another Kerry Chapman. I understand. One's expendable and the other isn't. That's why I'm agreeing to try."

Brett nodded. "Thanks."

Louise interrupted, saying, "I don't think you have to. Brett, my parents go caravanning all the time, you know. I used to go with them. I know a lot about caravans. All the touring ones are much the same these days. You can't see it from here but there's a compartment at the front – just above the towing gear. That's where they store the gas."

"Can you get at it from the outside?"

"Yes. That's the only way. You can't reach it from inside. But it'll be locked."

"Pity," he murmured. Then he brightened a little. "If the cylinder's not inside," he said, "the gas pipe must run underneath the caravan and up into it somewhere near the cooker."

"I think so," Louise said.

"That's it, then," Brett exclaimed. "If I can get underneath, I can break the pipe. No gas into the caravan, no explosion."

"I'll keep Robbie focused on the woman and the cooker," Naoki whispered. "That way, I can tell you if she starts anything."

Addressing Brett, Louise asked, "How are you going to get underneath without her knowing about it?"

Brett breathed in deeply, then exhaled. "I didn't say it would be easy," he said.

Louise gazed upwards and suggested, "You could wait for nightfall, I suppose."

Brett nodded. "I *could*, yes. And I will if necessary. But that's got its own problems. Like seeing the pipe in the dark. Like losing Robotroach's feedback if Dyer doesn't put a light on. I'd rather finish this business before it gets dark."

"You need a diversion," Louise suggested.

"Yes." Brett scrutinized his assistant. "Was that an offer?" He was desperate enough to clutch at any straw.

"I've got a lot to make up for," Louise said.

"OK." Quickly, Brett outlined his earlier exchange with Sophie. "So," he concluded, "you're a friend of mine with local knowledge. You could get out there and explain to Sophie that there's a hold-up. You've phoned Phil but he's stuck in an accident on the A630. It's blocked his way to the wood. That sort of thing. Plead for Kerry as well. Anything to keep her distracted. If Clare hears, she'll probably be able to move in as well, even if she doesn't know what we're up to. What do you think? Can you do that?"

Louise had her fingers crossed as she replied, "I'll give it a go."

Brett did not want to put the life of his god-daughter in the hands of a novice who'd already fouled up the rescue, but he had little choice. Perhaps his personal involvement in the case was blinding him to other options. But he needed a solution now and Louise was offering one. He knew from the Messenger case that she was plucky enough, but she was inexperienced. He wished that Clare was available instead. Yet he didn't have time for regret. "OK, Louise, it's you and me. Let's get on with it. And remember, I'm relying on you. Kerry's relying on you." He took a last lingering look at the computer screen. A debilitating melancholy seemed to have settled on the caravan. Unnaturally inert, Kerry's head had sagged on to her arms, which were resting on the table. Opposite her, Sophie stared out of each window, and at the ceiling, in turn. Occasionally she seemed to be staring at nothing at all. Sometimes she appeared nervous, as if expecting a cavalry charge on her caravan. "I'll get as close as I dare and then wave to you," Brett told Louise. "That's your signal to go up to the caravan and distract her. All right?"

Louise nodded. She felt too worried to reply.

Trying to convince himself as much as his young recruit, he said, "You can do it."

Brett soon found out what Clare already knew. Movement through the undergrowth was at best very difficult. At worst, it was impossible. The shambolic wood did not allow him free passage. It subjected him to nettle stings, bramble grazes, trips and thorn splinters. It denied him access to some places and demanded that he take circuitous routes. At last, though, he reached a spot that would allow him to approach the caravan without being seen from the door or the window alongside. He waved at Louise through the gathering gloom.

Louise gulped as if she were trying to swallow her unease and began to approach the caravan along the woodland trail.

Sophie did not waste any time. She saw Louise straightaway, jumped up and pushed open the window. "Where's Phil?" she shouted.

"I called him, like Brett told me to," Louise replied, not rushing her answer. She was trying to slow down the conversation to give Brett as much time as possible.

"Well?" Sophie asked impatiently.

Out of view, Brett disentangled himself from the clinging plants and crept towards the rear end of the caravan as fast as the wildlife would permit.

"I'm sorry," Louise was saying. "But he's stuck in traffic."

"Stuck in traffic? What do you mean?"

"Some sort of accident, apparently. It's blocked the A630. So he can't get here yet. But he's doing his best. He'll be here as soon as the road's cleared."

Suspiciously, Sophie snapped, "Where's Brett?"

"He's gone in our car to see what the hold-up is,"

Louise said from the track.

Brett cringed as he neared the hired mobile home. Even at a distance, Louise's deliberate response sounded like a lie. He hoped that Sophie was not very astute.

"And you're a friend of the Chapmans, are you?" Sophie checked.

"Only vaguely. I'm more a friend of Brett. I'm doing this because Brett asked me to."

"Do you know Kerry?"

The leading question made Brett hesitate. He hoped that Louise didn't fall into the trap. If she claimed that she knew Kerry, no doubt Sophie would push Kerry to the window and ask her to identify Louise. Brett bent down noiselessly and squeezed his body into the uncomfortably small gap between the rough ground and the caravan.

"No," Louise claimed. "I know of her, of course. That's all."

"Your friend, Brett Lawless," Sophie growled. "What is he?"

"What do you mean?" Louise asked, using delaying tactics.

"What's his job?" She was intent on testing Louise.

"He's a scientist," Louise answered, improvising well. "That's how he knows Phil. I think they met when they were studying. They both went to the same university. I'm not sure but it's something like that."

From beneath the caravan, Brett congratulated Louise silently.

Sophie nodded with an uneasy glint in her eye. She had suddenly realized that she had an unused resource and she disappeared from Louise's view.

Sophie's movement sounded like a thunderous drum in Brett's ears. It was dark and cramped under the caravan, but he could just make out a pipe running from the front to the left-hand side where the cooker was situated. Cautiously he touched it and found with dismay that it was made of metal. If he used all his strength, he would be able to bend the tube but it would not crack open. To stop the flow of gas, his only option was to try and dislodge the pipe from its fixing at one end. But any attempt to pull it out of its connection to the cylinder or to the cooker would require a phenomenal amount of power and cause a lot of noise. Before he could decide what to do, he heard Sophie's words filtering dully through the floor: "Kerry, tell me, what does Brett Lawless do? What's his job?"

Brett cursed. He didn't need Robotroach's camera to picture Kerry. He knew her well enough to imagine her reaction. She was a truthful girl. Faced with telling a lie, she would freeze. Her bewildered expression would tell Sophie all that she wanted to know.

Out of the window, Sophie snapped at Louise, "You're lying! You're the police. You haven't got Phil!"

Louise dodged the table knife that Sophie flung out of the window before she slammed it shut and secured the ratchet.

Brett heard Louise's gasp of horror and her retreating footsteps. Hidden underneath the caravan, he kept very quiet and listened for clues as to Sophie's next move. He feared what it would be.

She walked heavily to the centre of the caravan, directly above Brett. He couldn't pick out any sound by which to gauge Sophie's next action, but he could not mistake Kerry's alarm. "What are you doing?" his goddaughter cried. Then there was the noise that Brett had been dreading. It was so close to his ear that he could not mistake it. The hissing of gas through the pipe.

21

Wedged beneath the caravan, Brett felt as if he were tied to rails that hummed with the sound of an oncoming train. But he was thinking of Kerry.

Noise didn't matter any more. The only thing that mattered was stopping the flow of gas into the sealed caravan. He grasped the tubing in both hands and steeled himself.

From the wood, he heard another shout. Louise had also come to the conclusion that silence was no longer important. Using all her initiative, she yelled, "She's lit a candle, Brett. And the gas is on!"

How long would it take to fill the caravan with an explosive mixture of air and propane from the Calor gas cylinder? Brett didn't know, but he thought it wouldn't be long. He breathed in and then pulled with all his might on the pipe.

He felt it bend a little but knew immediately that he was wasting his time and energy. In the confined space, he could not apply all of his strength and the tube was securely attached at both ends. It would not budge. The gas continued to gush into the caravan. Brett muttered to himself and began to wriggle as quickly as he could to get out of the narrow cavity.

Above him, he could hear Kerry coughing and spluttering.

Struggling, he crawled out like an insect breaking free of its cramped pupal case. For a second he stood in front of the locked door. Even if he could barge his way through it, the rush of air could well speed the explosion. Breaking a window could do the same. Air might fan the flames.

No. He had to stop the Calor gas. Remembering Louise's advice, he dashed to the front of the caravan, glancing briefly through the window. In that moment, he saw Sophie and Kerry sitting on either side of the table. Between them, the small flame flickered brightly, evilly, in the dusk. It seemed to be waiting, hungry for more fuel before it flashed devastatingly throughout the caravan. Kerry had flopped on to the table. Was she out cold? Sophie was not paying any attention to Brett. She was preoccupied with her impending death. Her distant eyes told him that she regarded her fate as inevitable. She knew there was little that Brett could do with just seconds to go. Doubtless, she was pleased that the explosion would also destroy an interfering police officer.

On the tow-hitch body there was a Calor gas warning symbol. Brett wedged his fingertips behind the lip of the door to the compartment. But the panel was nearly flush against the side of the caravan. There wasn't enough of a gap to get a good grip. When he pulled, his fingers simply slipped off the door. He could not get enough leverage behind it to wrench it off its hinges, rip the fibreglass or shatter the two locks that held it in place.

Instead he looked around for a weapon. There was nothing that resembled a lever but a thick branch was lying on the ground. It would have to do. Frantically, he grabbed it and swung it with all his strength at the panel, like an enraged batsman thwacking a cricket ball. The wood crunched against the fibreglass and the impact sent a shudder through Brett's arms. The door cracked and buckled but did not give way. It was dented in the middle and the edges had sprung out under the pressure of Brett's blow.

Brett flung down the branch and applied his hands to the raised edges. This time he clasped the door securely. He took a deep breath and pulled. His muscles heaved. There was a ripping noise and the fibreglass split. The deformed panel sprang clear of the locks and the recoil sent Brett staggering back.

Inside the compartment, there were two Calor gas cylinders, one in use and a spare. Dropping the wrecked door, Brett strode up to them. He did not have the time to turn off the working cylinder. Instead, he grabbed the flexible tubing that led from the cylinder head to the metal fitting and yanked it away.

Immediately, the gas hissed at him like an angry animal, but at least he had broken the connection. No more gas flooded into the caravan. But there was still enough propane in the enclosed space to blast the caravan, and it occupants, to the tree tops. Brett had done what he could. Now it was up to Kerry. To rouse her, he yelled at the top of his voice, "Kerry! Blow out the candle!"

At the sound of a familiar voice, Kerry perked up. She was jolted into doing what she was told without question. She blew and coughed at the same time. Sophie did not emerge from her reverie quickly enough to cup the flame protectively with her hands. It bent over and died. A wisp of grey smoke twirled above the extinguished, blackened wick.

Brett bent down, leaned into the compartment and turned off the gas at the valve. By the time that he was upright again, he was faced with an unexpected and appalling sight. He had thought it was all over. He had thought that he had won. But he was wrong. Sophie was not ready to be arrested and taken away. Brett shivered with shock.

Behind the window, Sophie had one arm around Kerry's neck; in the other she held aloft a long serrated bread knife. She gave a loud demented cackle.

"No!" Brett yelled. Yet he was helpless. The windows were sealed from the inside and he knew that the door was locked. He could do nothing.

Suddenly, there was the dramatic crash of splintering glass from the left-hand side of the caravan. In one swift movement, Clare's fist smashed through the window behind Sophie and snatched the kitchen knife from her unsuspecting hand. Before Sophie, Brett or Kerry could react to her intervention, Clare had removed the knife from the caravan and, wincing, dropped it on the ground. Drops of blood splashed on to the bright blade. With extraordinary courage Clare aimed a second blow with her injured fist. Striking between the sharp glass teeth that still protruded from the window frame, her ferocious punch caught Sophie, still stunned, on the neck.

Kerry screamed.

At once, Sophie was winded. Abruptly, her right arm slipped from Kerry's shoulders and she slumped drunkenly across the table like a boxer, battered senseless, collapsing to the canvas with a sickening thud. The proficient jab, the foul air and the trauma of Clare's awesome attack had finished her.

Taking the long route to the front door, Brett saw Clare. His partner was steady on her feet but startled by her own audacity and her injuries. She was losing a copious amount of blood from a hideous slit up her right arm. He put a hand briefly on her shoulder and squeezed. "Louise!" he shouted into the wood. "Help Clare!" Then he dashed to the door.

He knew how to do it. During their last case Clare

had told him how the Messenger was able to fracture bones by kicking with his foot and she had just demonstrated the same strength. He knew that, if he wanted to crash through the door, it was no use focusing on the door itself and aiming to barge it with his shoulder. He had to concentrate on a point inside the caravan, just like Clare had fixed her eye on the woman behind the glass and struck as if the window weren't there. Standing back, he hesitated, to gather his strength and resolve. Yet he could not match Clare's self-confidence and prowess. It wasn't easy to think of a target beyond when the door was right there in front of him, solid and obvious. He braced himself, thought of Kerry and ran at the caravan. He concentrated on charging straight through it.

Brett flung himself into the door with a fearful crushing noise. The fibreglass dented and the door bowed but it stayed in place. Rebounding, Brett glared at it angrily, inhaled and then slammed his foot into the weakened structure. The handle and lock crumpled and the door sprang open, emitting a rush of Calor gas.

Brett leapt inside the gloomy caravan and dived towards Kerry.

She exclaimed, "Brett!" Then she threw her one free arm around his big shoulders and hugged him.

"It's going to be all right, Kerry," he whispered in her ear. "I've come to take you home."

Kerry could not speak. She was too shocked.

Gripping him fervently and unable to let go, she kept repeating, "Brett. Brett."

He reassured her again but Kerry would not calm down. Then he realized that she had been scared not by Sophie's threat, but by Clare's display of unnerving violence. While Brett admired the brutal self-sacrifice and intense power that Clare had summoned, Kerry had been terrified by it. "It's OK," Brett murmured. "It was Clare, a police officer like me, come to rescue you. She's a friend. I'm proud of her. And she saved you. Everything's going to be all right."

Kerry sniffed and whimpered, "It was horrible."

Brett was not sure if she was referring to the whole kidnap ordeal or to Clare's extreme act but at least she was talking normally, making sense. Brett felt a flood of relief. While he hugged Kerry, he experienced sudden exhaustion and elation in equal measure. "You've been very brave," he told her. "Now, it's time to go home. Your mum and dad are waiting for you. They've been so worried about you. You know," he added, "I'm not sure they've been as brave as you, but don't tell them I said so, will you? I don't want to get into trouble." He felt Kerry shake her head. He untangled himself from her and said, "Let me find the key to this lock and get you freed."

Brett did not realize how dark it had become until he saw the lights of the police cars snaking down the track. Sophie had regained consciousness but still seemed dazed. She looked down at her hands, secured with her own device made from a bike chain, and moaned. Brett arrested her and recited, "You do not have to say anything. But it may harm your defence if you do not mention, when questioned, something which you later rely on in court. Anything you do say may be given in evidence." While he was cautioning her, she gazed into his face as if he were a ghost. Brett sent her back to Sheffield in the first car with two restraining officers.

Then Brett guided Kerry out of the caravan. Just before she reached the door, she pointed to the floor by the bottom bunk and squealed, "Ugh! Look!" She raised her foot to stamp on a horrid insect.

Brett's hands under Kerry's arms lifted her easily off her feet and her leg flailed in mid-air. Putting her down and turning her round, Brett squatted in front of her and explained, "Maybe it doesn't look very pretty, like Clare's punch, but it saved your life as well. Your dad knows the man who made it. He's outside. A very clever man."

Kerry frowned. "Bet he's not as clever as my dad," she said indignantly.

Brett chuckled. "Maybe not, but your dad owes him a lot. So I think we'd better not stamp on his insect, eh? What do you think?"

"I don't like insects," Kerry declared.

Brett smiled. "In the car, I'll tell you all about this one. Then I think you'll change your mind. It's very special. It's even got a name – Robbie."

At the edge of the track, Clare and Louise were

standing together. Louise had torn the sleeves from her blouse and used them to bind Clare's wounds tightly to prevent further loss of blood. The cloth had turned a sickly shade of red. "All right?" Brett asked his partner.

Clare nodded shakily.

Kerry was still wary of Clare and edged away from her.

"If you weren't sunburnt, you'd be as white as a sheet," Brett said. "The next car's yours. Taxi to hospital to have your punctures repaired."

"Very funny," Clare mumbled.

Brett arranged for another driver to take Naoki back to the university as soon as the technologist had collected together his equipment and shut down the system. Brett apologized to him, saying, "I hope you don't mind someone else driving you back. I want to take Kerry straight to her own house. I'm sure you understand."

"Of course," he replied.

"And thanks," Brett added. "I owe you one. I can't tell you how useful you've been. You and Robbie."

Naoki smiled triumphantly. "You don't have to. I saw for myself how helpful I've been. I *can* tell, and I will. Tell everyone." He could hardly contain his exuberance. He held out his hand, palm upwards. "It's going to rain soon – rain funds."

Almost as soon as Brett pulled up outside Kerry's home, the front door of the house opened. With his arm round Kerry's shoulder, Brett had not even escorted her across the pavement when two exhilarated people and one ecstatic dog bounded down the garden path.

Brett stood back and allowed the Chapman family to rejoice in its reunion. Feverishly, Chloe embraced her daughter and stroked her untidy hair. Copper ran round and round, barking joyously. In the yellow glow from the streetlight, Phil nodded at Brett, a gesture that expressed more gratitude than any words he could produce amid such emotion, and joined in the tearful scrum.

Brett did not stay long. It was a time for the Chapmans to indulge themselves on their own. Announcing that he'd call round in the morning to tell them the full story, he sped away to the hospital.

22

There had been a transformation of epic proportions at the Chapmans' house. Friday morning was like Christmas day without presents. The bleak, restless mood had been displaced by celebration. Brett did not want to spoil the occasion so he galloped through Thursday evening's events as quickly as he could.

"I'd better go and see Naoki Matsumoto," Phil declared after listening to Brett. "I've got a lot to thank him for."

"Is Clare all right?" Chloe enquired urgently, concerned for one of her daughter's saviours.

"She's been worse. Some cuts and one nasty gash but she's patched up and back at work. She'll be fine."

With a kindly expression Phil said, "You and

Clare. You make a natural pair."

"Yeah," Brett agreed. "She's quite something. We seem to make good partners."

Phil groaned. "Always the police officer!" Smiling mischievously, he added, "I wasn't talking law and order. You make a good couple. Think about it."

Brett shook his head wryly. "I have thought about it. But I doubt if Clare has."

"Want a fiver on it?" Phil retorted cheekily. "Don't underestimate yourself, Brett. She's human. And she gets on with you. That's obvious."

Resisting Phil's suggestion, Brett dictated the official line. "In police work, we've got to respect each other. That's for sure. But anything more is positively dangerous. We go into a job with our minds on the public, not on each other."

Perceptively, Phil replied, "That's just the boss speaking." He continued, "At work, I like to think I'm in control of chemical reactions but I can't over-rule thermodynamics. I can't stop some chemicals reacting even if I want to. I mix them and they're away. Nothing I can do about it. I can't hold them back. No matter what the boss says, they'll react and that's that. It's called nature."

Kerry looked up at Brett and said, "Promise you'll be careful. Your girlfriend, Brett, she's dangerous, as well as pretty."

Brett knelt down in front of Kerry and replied, "I promise. But she's not dangerous to me. Now, it's time you started worrying about your mum and dad, not me. Believe me, they were lost without you. They need looking after."

At lunchtime, Brett drove Clare to her favourite restaurant in Hathersage. Her right hand and arm were bandaged right up to the elbow to hold together the stitches in the long ugly tear. At the table, she manipulated her knife awkwardly but she was enjoying the meal anyway. She washed it down with real ale. "Getting injured has its compensations," she said, "if you treat me like this. You haven't even grumbled about me eating fish. Amazing. And you're paying as well. Incredible."

Brett smiled weakly. There was something on his mind. He put down his knife and fork and asked her bluntly, "Clare, are you still tempted by Jack Fitzgerald's game? Art theft? Have you got a transfer in mind? Don't deny that you haven't thought about it."

"No, I don't deny it," Clare answered. Following Brett's example, she stopped eating. "When I see a painting I like, I get that tingle in my spine. When I hear about them being nicked, I get angry. Yes, I'd like to tackle art theft. But, I don't know, I suppose I saw you coming out of that caravan with Kerry, saw her face, and I knew I was doing the right job already. You don't get adrenalin like that when you recover a stolen painting."

Brett nodded with heartfelt relief. "Good," he said.

"Except that's not the whole story," she added. "The real reason is, I couldn't work with a superior who refers to his *lasses*."

Brett laughed freely. "I thought Fitzgerald had blown it as soon as I heard him say that. I knew you'd never forgive him."

In the afternoon, Brett and Clare were called to the chief's office. Brett's eyebrows rose and Louise began to quake. On her way out, Clare put her good hand on Louise's shoulder and smiled. "It'll be OK," she whispered. "We've all made much worse mistakes."

John Macfarlane put his mug of coffee down on the desk beside Brett's report and nodded towards Clare's strapped arm. "All right?" he enquired.

Clare nodded.

"How does it feel?"

"Sore but I'm fine."

"Mmm." Big John contemplated the investigation and said, "It shouldn't have happened, though. Avoidable. A right old shambles at the end, all due to Louise Jenson's clanger. A literal clanger."

"I took her along to liaise," Brett said, using an argument that he had rehearsed. "She liaised by phone, as she was told. I didn't tell her to turn it off in the wood."

"So it's your fault! Is that the line you're selling me?" The chief laughed with a hint of mockery. "Very noble, but she shouldn't have to be told. It only requires a bit of intelligence. It's a blot on her record."

"I know," Brett replied. "But there's plenty of good stuff in her record as well. Give her a person to contact, a fact to find and a phone, and it's as good as done."

"Mmm," John murmured. "I'll take it into account while I think about her position." Changing the subject, he grumbled, "That's not the only complaint. I got a note from the Fire and Rescue Service about you."

"Ah, yes."

"I explained it away."

"How?"

"By telling them an enthusiastic officer can overstep the mark and get impetuous. By telling them I'd reprimand you. So, consider yourself reprimanded, and hope they've forgotten about it before you come across them again." He stared severely at both of them and continued, "And I can see a couple of bills coming my way. For repairs to a door and for a busted caravan. Very busted. But there's another important issue in here. Another clanger, of the type that you, Clare, were there to prevent. You're the one with the common sense and experience. I told you to hold his hand and keep him out of trouble." John's fleshy fingers touched the top page of the report. "There seems to be a discrepancy between the time you went into Dyer's house and the time the search warrant was issued. How do you explain that one? Watch playing up, was it?"

"Clare did warn me but I went in straightaway on the basis that it could've saved Kerry's life or prevented serious injury to her."

"Ah, I see," John retorted showily. "You had reason to believe she was in the house, then?"

Brett glanced out of the window and took a deep breath.

Before he could answer, John said, "I'll take that as a yes." Smiling at Brett and tossing the papers back at him, he added, "So, put it in the report and it's all done." His tone fell neatly between annoyance and endorsement.

"Thank you, sir," Brett replied. "And Louise? You're recommending…?"

John grimaced at the telephone as its ringing interrupted them. "Hang on, you two," he ordered as he picked up the receiver. Answering the call brusquely, he barked, "Macfarlane". He drummed his fingers on his desk, listened for a few seconds and then muttered, "A fire. What's it got to do with me? Hasn't the fire brigade squirted water on it?" John's fingers froze. "I see. Unpleasant. Very unpleasant. Where is it?" After noting the reply, John looked at Brett and Clare across the desk as he announced into the telephone, "Yeah, I've got someone here who'll take it on. The perfect team."